+
Sa14u

UNDERDOG

UNDERDOG

Marilyn Sachs

DOUBLEDAY & COMPANY, INC.
Garden City, New York

Library of Congress Cataloging in Publication Data

Sachs, Marilyn.
  Underdog.

  Summary: Lonely, confused, and in need of love in her new
life with an aunt and uncle in San Francisco, a twelve-year-old
orphan searches for her long-lost dog.
  [1. Orphans—Fiction. 2. Dogs—Fiction] I. Title.
PZ7.S1187Un 1985   [Fic]
ISBN: 0-385-17609-0

Library of Congress Catalog Card Number 84-24676

With love to Paul who will not read
a story about a dog who dies.

1

"Your father," Sandy said, helping herself to a piece of pepperoni pizza, "was the finest man in the world." She had tears in her eyes as she laid the piece on her plate and began folding it inward. "Nobody cared the way he did. He was always on the side of the underdog."

She looked at me across the table before she raised the piece to her mouth. "You can be proud of him, Izzy. There are very few girls who ever had a father like yours."

I watched her as she chewed on the pizza, and I nodded and tried not to look anxious. I had been staying with Sandy ever since my father died over a week ago, but she still had not said what I was waiting to hear.

Sandy was the first one I called when I woke up that morning and didn't find him home. It was Saturday and the house was very quiet. My father never slept late, even on the weekends. I always heard him before I got out of bed and I usually jumped up and got dressed quickly. I never wanted him to think I was lazy. I hadn't seen him the night before but that didn't make me suspicious. He often stayed out late and I went to sleep when I was tired. Now that I was eleven, I didn't need Mrs. Evans to baby-sit unless my father didn't expect to be home all night.

It's not a good feeling waking up alone in the morning even for somebody like me. I called Sandy. She said, "Oh, Izzy darling, oh, Izzy!"

"Dad's not home," I told her. "Maybe he went out already but I don't think he's been home all night."

"Oh, Izzy!" Sandy said. "I can't believe it. You mean nobody's told you?"

She came right over and took me back with her. My father had died in a car crash. He was on his way to court and Sandy said it still wasn't clear who had been speeding or who had lost control but he had been in a coma all night at the hospital and she had been with him, waiting, hoping, until the very end. She had just come through the door of her apartment, as a matter of fact, when she heard the phone ringing. "Oh, Izzy," she said, "he never regained consciousness. Once I thought his eyes fluttered. He made a little face as if he was in pain but the doctor said he didn't feel a thing."

She cried a lot that week even though she and my father had been divorced over three years ago and he had been married to and divorced from Karen in the meantime. I didn't much like Karen but I loved Sandy and she loved me. I could talk to her on the telephone whenever I liked and stay over at her house when my father was away on business. She always said she felt as if she were my real mother and I believed her. Now, as we sat in the restaurant eating our pepperoni pizza, I waited for her to say it again.

"Have some more pizza, Izzy," she said. "You're not eating anything."

How beautiful Sandy was with her long black hair and large gray eyes! She put out her hand and pressed mine. Her fingernails were broken and caked with the dyes she used on her candles. That morning, she had made five dozen red, orange, and green tulip candles that she hoped to sell before Easter. As long as I could remember, Sandy smelled of candles, and when I leaned against her or she kissed me the fragrance of wax was always in her hair.

"Poor Izzy," Sandy said, her eyes filling with tears. "What will you do now?"

For the first time since my father died, I felt frightened. All along I had believed that Sandy wanted me. If she really loved me as she always said she did, if she really felt toward me as a mother, wouldn't she ask me to come and live with her now? I wouldn't bother her, she knew that. I was used to taking care of myself. I could help her make her candles, and I could take the laundries to the laundromat and wait there if Sandy needed some time to herself. I wouldn't bother her. I was good at not bothering people. Even my father always said so. And I could go with Sandy on weekends to the street fairs and sit there and sell her candles if she wanted to take a walk or go have a cup of coffee somewhere. I could be useful to Sandy.

"I'm going back to school," Sandy said.

"School?" I repeated.

"Uh-huh," Sandy said. "Candles are dead. I can't live on candles anymore. Nobody buys candles."

I thought of Sandy's wonderful, bright, messy apartment with candles everywhere—spiraled candles, square candles, big ones, little ones. Candles shaped like hearts and pineapples and candles speckled with gold or striped red, white, and blue. It wouldn't be Sandy without her candles.

"Computers," Sandy said. "That's where all the action is now. I'm going into computers. I want to change my life-style."

"No!" I cried. "Don't change your life-style. Please, Sandy! I love your candles. I love you. I want to come and live with you. I can help you with the candles. I can do the laundries. I can shop . . ."

Sandy burst into tears. "Oh, Izzy," she cried, "oh, Izzy, darling Izzy!" She put her head down on the table and began crying so hard, her shoulders shook all over the place. So I got up, came around to her side of the booth and tried to comfort her. She put her arms around me— her hair smelled of wax—and began kissing me and kissing me. Her tears ran down my cheeks as well as her own. She said she would always love me and whatever happened I could always count on her to be there when I needed her, but that it was absolutely impossible for me to come and live with her.

I went to see Karen the next day. Jeremy, my little half brother, was getting a new tooth and Karen complained about it the same way she had complained about every single tooth of Jeremy's as it arrived. She also complained about her back, the price of grapefruits, and the weather. Then she went to work on Sandy.

"Why they called her from the office before they called me, I'd like to know," she said.

"Nobody called me," I murmured.

"Okay, it was impossible for me to get over to the hospital. Jeremy was feverish and I couldn't get a sitter but if Mark wanted to see anybody before he died it would have been me. Even if we were divorced, we were still good friends and, you know, Izzy, he was a devoted father and always came to see Jeremy whenever he had any free time."

"Well, he never regained consciousness," I told her.

"Oh sure," Karen said, "you always stick up for Sandy."

She was glaring at me and I got that kind of silly, helpless smile on my face when somebody is acting stupid and you know it and she knows it and you feel sorry for her and sorry for yourself but there's no way to make things better.

Luckily, Jeremy started yelling and we both hurried into his bedroom where he was standing up in his crib, screaming and shaking the bars. A big, husky kid with fat red cheeks and pale hair just like Karen's. I never felt much of anything about Jeremy. I didn't love him and I didn't hate him. I certainly wasn't jealous of him. My father never gave him any more attention than he gave me and the poor kid and his mother were out of our house almost as soon as he was born.

"Hey, Jersey, Jersey, Jersey!" I cooed at him and he stopped yelling and began grinning and holding out his arms. I picked him up and the smell from inside his diapers nearly knocked me over. But I bobbled him up and down before Karen took him from me and laid him down to change his diapers.

"Boo, boo, boo!" I crooned at him and he giggled away and kicked his feet.

"You really have a way with him," Karen said, inspecting the contents of his diapers.

"Boo, boo, boo!" I continued.

Naturally, I wanted Karen to think I had a way with him. I wanted her to tell me I could come and live with her and Jeremy. If Sandy didn't want me, Karen and Jeremy were the only other possibilities I could think of.

"But isn't it amazing how he always knows you?" Karen said. "Ever since he was a tiny infant he's known who was who and when Mark used to come over . . . oh . . . oh!" Karen began crying and I patted her on the shoulder and murmured something comforting.

After a while we moved into the living room and Karen sat Jeremy down on the carpet and gave him some plastic rings to chew on. Then she started complaining about the way my father hadn't had a proper funeral.

"Nobody asked me what I thought," she said.

"Well, I guess he must have told everybody that he didn't want a funeral. Sandy says there's going to be a memorial service as soon as the other lawyers can arrange it."

I could see she was getting irritated again so I slipped down on the floor and began playing with the baby. When I looked up at her, Karen almost smiled at me.

"I guess you're all settled in at Sandy's," she said suddenly. "I guess you don't need anything."

It wasn't really a question but I made sure to answer it.

"Well, no," I told her. "I'm not really settled in. It's only for a while until . . . I mean, Sandy's going back to school so I can't stay with her."

I could see the almost smile fading and I quickly put my hands over my eyes and said, "Boo, boo!" to Jeremy. He laughed and laughed and when I looked up at Karen again, she was frowning.

"That Sandy has got to be the most selfish person in the whole world," she said to me.

"Boo!" I said to the baby.

"She never thinks of anybody but herself. I don't know why Mark ever married her. I guess he was sorry for her. You know him—he was sorry for everybody."

"Boo!"

But then she stopped complaining and started talking to me. So I sat back up on the chair and listened to her.

"I'm sorry," she said. "I can't."

I knew what she meant so I asked her, "Why not? I wouldn't be any trouble. I'd help you with Jeremy and I could do the cooking."

"You don't know how to cook," she said, looking at me as if she was thinking it over. "Mrs. Evans does the cooking."

"Not always," I said quickly. "Not on weekends. She doesn't come in on weekends so I could do it. And I don't eat much and I'm not picky. Even Dad always said I'd eat anything that stayed still on my plate. And Mrs. Evans said I help her a lot and that I'm much neater than most kids my age."

"I know," Karen said mournfully. "You do. You're very

neat and you don't get into trouble. You're a good child. I know that, Izzy."

My mouth stopped right where it was. Karen had never said anything really nice about me before. This was the first time. I began smiling. She almost smiled back at me.

I could feel the panic easing. Maybe I'd even grow to like her one of these days. "Boo!" I said to the baby.

"I'm sorry," Karen said again, "but I can't take you."

I must have looked as if I was going to fall apart because suddenly she turned her eyes away from me and went on talking very quickly. "I can't do it, Izzy, because . . . I know you're going to find this hard to believe but I'm getting married again."

"Married?"

"I was just getting around to telling your father before the accident—well—it's a neighbor, Jim Franklin. He's got two little girls. One is Jeremy's age and the other is about three. His wife died about a year ago. I didn't know her because he moved here after she died. He's been frantic taking care of the kids and working, so I've tried to help out. He's a good man, an accountant—nothing like your father. Nobody's like your father. But he's a kind man and I'm tired of being alone."

"I can help with the kids," I said. "You know I'm good with kids. You always said so yourself."

She gave me a quick pat on my head and said, without looking at me, "I'm sorry, Izzy. I'm really sorry."

After a while she began complaining about Sandy again, how Sandy should be the one to take me because I always loved her the best. I interrupted her. I was so frightened now I could feel it up behind my ears. "So what will happen to me?" I asked her. "Where will I go?"

"I guess to your uncle in San Francisco," she told me.

2

I had forgotten about my uncle.

Forgotten wasn't exactly the right word since I hadn't really ever known him. When we left San Francisco, I had been four and my memories of all my relatives were dim. All I really knew was that we had left right after my mother's death and that my father wasn't on speaking terms with his brother.

"They never really got along," Sandy once told me. "I think your uncle was always jealous of your father. Of course he's a lawyer too and he makes a lot of money but he's not a famous lawyer like your father. And he doesn't stand up for good causes or help people who really need him. He's only interested in the almighty dollar. I'm sure that's why they quarreled."

My uncle was sitting in Sandy's living room one afternoon when I came home from school. He stood up when I came into the room and Sandy said in a phony voice, "Here's your Uncle Roger from San Francisco, Izzy."

"Izzy?" my uncle said.

"Short for Isabelle," Sandy told him. "Isn't that what she was always called?"

"I don't remember," he said, trying to smile at me. He was taller than my father and thinner, and his clothes looked much neater. "Hello, Izzy," he said, and just stayed where he was.

"Hello," I said back to him. I didn't know what I was supposed to do then so I just stayed where I was and nodded my head at him a couple of times and felt stupid.

Finally he moved over to me and put an arm around my shoulder and gave it a quick, nervous little squeeze. "You look a lot like your father," he told me.

"Oh, do you really think so?" Sandy said. "Mark wasn't as dark and she has a longer face."

"Well." He took his arm off my shoulder and moved back. "Of course the last time I saw Mark was seven years ago but it seems to me she looks very much like him."

"She looks more like you, I think," Sandy said in that phony, buttery voice. I knew she was trying to soften my uncle up, trying to get him to like me so he would take me away with him.

Sandy helped me pack my things and she kept laughing and yattering and saying how she would be out to San Francisco to see me and how I could come back to Washington, D.C., to visit her anytime. She gave me one of her most beautiful candles—a jade-green castle candle with little turrets and she kept kissing me and kissing me.

When we were ready to go the tears rolled down her cheeks but I didn't cry.

My uncle and I stayed in my father's apartment until we left. I had to go through two more times with Sandy— once after the memorial service for my father and then again at the airport. She came running into the waiting room just a few minutes before we boarded the plane with more tears and kisses and another candle, shaped like a tree with red heart blossoms.

Karen didn't come to the airport. After the memorial service she had gone on and on to my uncle, complaining about the mess my father had left his affairs in.

"I told him over and over again to write out a will," she said, "but he was always too busy. He never had a minute to himself. 'Charity begins at home,' I kept telling him but, no, any crazy radical nut group who needed a free lawyer or any battered wife or abused orphan who wanted advice—he always had time for them but for his own wife and son . . ."

"I'm sure it will all work out," my uncle told her politely. "You'd be surprised how many lawyers neglect to write wills for themselves, but after we get it all sorted out there should be something left for you and the children."

"Children?" she asked, surprised.

"Yes—Jeremy and Isabelle."

"Oh—yes—Isabelle." That was when she remembered me, and she gave me a quick kiss and wished me good luck in San Francisco before she started complaining again to my uncle.

He had been too busy the last days we spent in Washington, D.C., to do much talking to me. He told me to pack what I needed and said something about trying not to bring too much. But he was surprised when he saw that I'd managed to get everything into two suitcases.

"Is this all?" he asked.

I wanted to please him. All I wanted then was for him to be pleased. "Is that all right?" I asked him. "If you think it's too much, I can dump a few more things."

"No, no," he said. "I don't want you to leave anything that's meaningful."

I smiled as brightly as I could and said, "I took some clothes and books and a few odds and ends. I don't need anything else. I didn't want to take too much, just like you said."

"But Isabelle—Izzy—I only meant that you couldn't bring too many large things but I certainly wouldn't want you to leave important mementos or toys that you're fond of."

Toys? I kept smiling.

". . . or presents your father gave you."

"He usually gave me money. Once I bought myself this silver charm bracelet. The one I'm wearing." I showed it to him. "And once I bought a camera. But I'm taking that."

"Are you sure, Izzy," he asked gravely, "that this is all you want to take?"

"I'm sure," I told him.

On the airplane, he tried to begin a real conversation but it was tough going for both of us.

"You were just a little girl when you left San Francisco," he said, "and we never really got to know you."

"Oh, that's all right," I said.

"Your Aunt Alice and I were really shocked when your stepmother called us and told us about your father."

"Uh—which stepmother?" I asked him.

"The one with the baby," he said. "The second one."

"Oh, Karen."

"Yes, that's right, Karen." He cleared his throat and started out again. "Izzy, I think you should know that your father and I weren't on speaking terms."

"Oh, that's okay. Lots of people weren't on speaking terms with my father."

"It's not what you probably think," he said, and then he stopped. "What do you think?" he asked, sounding kind of confused.

I told him. "Sandy said—you know—Sandy, my first stepmother. The one with the candles. She thought maybe it had to do with—well—both of you are lawyers and you make a lot of money and maybe you didn't approve of all the causes that he was always involved in and that he never made much money on."

"Oh no," my uncle said. "It wasn't that."

"It's okay," I said quickly. "It doesn't matter." I didn't want my uncle to think I took my father's side. My father was dead and if my uncle didn't let me stay with him, I knew that would be the end of the line for me. My mother had been an only child and both sets of grandparents were dead.

"Your father and I quarreled a great deal," my uncle said in his slow, grave voice. "I can't deny that we did, Izzy. We quarreled as boys and as men but the one thing we never quarreled over was our differences as lawyers. I was always—am now—proud of what he stood for. Izzy, your father was a brave fighter for human rights."

"I know," I told him. "He was for the underdog."

I don't think he heard me. His face creased up in solemn wrinkles. "No, it wasn't what you think at all. This last, worst quarrel had to do with . . ." He looked right at me and shook his head. "Izzy, it had to do with your mother's death."

"It's okay," I tried to reassure him. I didn't know much about my mother's death. Only that it had happened when I was four and that she had fallen and broken her neck in a freak accident. But she was dead too and I didn't want my uncle to think I was on her side either.

"Your father—I don't know what he ever said to you about that."

"Not much," I told him. "He never talked about my mother. Sometimes he talked about Sandy and sometimes he talked about Karen but he never said anything about my mother."

"Did he . . . did he ever say anything about me?" My uncle leaned toward me and watched my face. He wanted me to say something and I wanted to say it. But I wasn't sure what it was. I couldn't remember my father ever saying anything about my uncle.

"Nothing bad," I told him. "He never said anything bad about you."

"Oh!" My uncle straightened up. "Well, Izzy, maybe one day if you're interested we could talk about it." He began mumbling how he supposed since I was only eleven we could wait a few years.

"No hurry," I assured him.

Then he said how my Aunt Alice, that's his wife, was anxious to see me again. How she really wanted to come to Washington for the memorial service but how somebody got sick in the art gallery where she works and they couldn't find a replacement.

"That's okay," I told him.

Aunt Alice opened the door when we arrived at their condominium. I'm still not sure what a condominium is but they had a great big one with lots of rooms and views of the city from every window you looked out of. All the furniture and rugs were white or off-white and each room had big ugly paintings hanging on the walls and big ugly statues standing on the floor that made you want to say yuk. The best part was outside the windows where you could look at the tops of houses, the ships sailing on the bay, and the big bridge with the little cars going back and forth.

I didn't say yuk. I smiled at Aunt Alice and when she bent down to kiss me I smelled an unfamiliar perfume in her hair and I had to hold on hard to my smile to keep from crying.

"We're so happy to have you here, Isabelle," said my aunt.

"Izzy," my uncle corrected. "They all call her Izzy."

"Izzy, dear," said my aunt, "we're so happy to have you here."

"I'm happy to be here," I told her.

My aunt matched the apartment. All her clothes seemed to be white or off-white and her face was pale and her hair was frosted.

We all stood there smiling at each other for a while and

then she said she supposed I'd like to see the room I'd be sleeping in. She didn't say it was my room but I said yes, I would like to see it. Then we all trooped off to a room that had a bed with a white bedspread on it and some even uglier paintings on the wall.

"This is our guest room," Aunt Alice told me.

"Oh, it's very nice," I said, trying to sound enthusiastic.

"I thought you'd like it," she said. "That painting facing the bed with the lovely azures and gentians always makes me want to cry."

It made me want to cry too. I didn't know what azures and gentians meant but the thought of waking up every morning and facing that wall full of big blue spots and splashes like pigeon droppings made me want to scream.

"And come over here to the window, Izzy," said my uncle. "I think the view from this window is the best in the whole place. Look over there. That's Market Street and there's the Ferry Building. Later when it gets dark you'll have thousands of lights twinkling up at you."

I murmured something and kept smiling but all I wanted was for them to leave me alone so I could cry. I hadn't had a chance, I'd been so busy worrying in the past few weeks. I needed to cry now and I needed to be alone.

"So, Izzy," said my aunt, "why don't you wash up? You have your own bathroom right there across the room. I fixed an early dinner because I assumed your stomach would still be on Eastern time."

"Oh, I'm not hungry," I told her. "We had a big lunch on the plane and I never eat much anyway."

"Well, whatever you like," said my aunt, and she and my uncle walked out of the room. They didn't close the door after them. I wanted to close the door but I also didn't want them to think I was sneaky or secretive so I left it open and made a dash for the bathroom where I could close the door. Naturally it was tiled all in white and I fell down on the white floor and cried. I threw a few towels around too. They were pale pink which should have made me feel better but it didn't. Then I threw up the lunch I had eaten on the plane. After that, I picked up the towels, washed my face, splashed a lot of water on my eyes, combed my hair, stretched my mouth into a smile, and joined my aunt and uncle in the dining room.

They were talking in whispers as I came into the room but as soon as they saw me they raised their voices and began smiling.

"You know, Izzy, I think you look just like your father," said my aunt.

"That's exactly what I think too," said my uncle, "but— uh—somebody I said that to . . ."

"Sandy," I told him.

"Yes, that's right. Sandy said she thought Izzy looked more like me."

"Oh no," said my aunt. "Her face is longer, like Mark's, and she's darker than you are."

I agreed, and soon we were sitting down to dinner around the fanciest table I'd ever seen in my life. In the center stood one perfect flower surrounded by two long, skinny, translucent candles—nothing like Sandy's—in two spiky silver candlesticks. All the plates naturally were white but the food was arranged so beautifully on each one I could hardly believe you were supposed to eat it.

"Go ahead, Izzy," said my aunt. "I'm sure you're hungry."

And suddenly I was. Not only because I wanted to please her but because I really was hungry and the food tasted so wonderful. I ate and smiled and ate and smiled until suddenly my aunt started talking about schools.

". . . boarding schools," she was saying.

I stopped eating.

". . . not now, of course," she said. "It's too late this year but in the fall. We'll have lots of time over the summer, Izzy, to look over the catalogs and maybe visit a few. We don't want you to be too far away, after all. We want to come and see you and you'll want to spend some of your holidays with us . . ."

So it wasn't going to be my room after all. Aunt Alice had made a chocolate mousse for dessert but I couldn't eat any.

3

Well, I told myself the next morning when I woke up and saw the painting of blue pigeon droppings on the opposite wall, at least I won't have to see that every morning if I'm not living here.

In a way, I felt relieved but not happy. It was the end of the line. I couldn't go any further so that was a relief. But it wasn't good knowing that nobody wanted me and that I had to go to boarding school.

Cheer up, I told myself after I had washed up and stood looking around the (not my) room. Keep busy. Don't mope or they might get rid of you even sooner. This is only the middle of April so you do have at least four months before they ship you off. It's even possible if you make a good impression that they might change their minds.

I opened the door of my room and listened. No sounds

out there. It was Sunday morning. I was used to my father's early hours and the clock in my room said 8:15.
Some people, I supposed, slept late on Sunday morning.
Gently, I closed the door and decided to remain in my
room until I heard wake-up noises from outside.

My two suitcases stood in the middle of the room. I
guessed it would be okay to unpack. Last night, Aunt Alice
had said I should and that, for the time being, I could hang
my clothes in the big closet in the room and use the
double chests for anything that folded. I didn't need all
that space. My underwear, sweaters, and socks fitted into
one of the chests with lots of room to spare and when I
finished hanging up the rest of my clothes, a whole long
row of empty hangers still remained. The closet was one
of those interesting ones with shelves and hooks and bars
if I could only figure out what they were meant for. I laid
my pair of tennis shoes and my boots on a slanting wire
stand on the closet floor and hoped it was intended for
shoes. I decided to put my books on the shelves. One of
them had a big box sitting on it.

Aunt Alice knocked on my door and waited until I said
"Come in" before she opened it.

"Oh, my," she said, "you really are an early bird. Do you
always get up early on weekends or are you just still on
Eastern time?"

"I guess I'm used to getting up early," I said. "But I can
be very quiet."

She was wearing a shimmering white bathrobe and her
hair looked combed. "We're kind of lazy," she explained,
"over the weekends. Especially on Sundays. Roger—your
Uncle Roger—likes to loaf and just read the paper."

"I can stay in this room," I said. "I don't want to bother you."

Aunt Alice shook her head. "No, Izzy, I don't want you to feel that way . . . I . . ." She didn't finish what she was going to say. Instead she walked over to the closet and looked inside.

"Is this everything?" she asked.

"I put all the rest in the chest and my shoes are on that rack. That's meant for shoes, isn't it?"

"Oh yes," my aunt said, looking at my two pairs of shoes. "Don't you have any more shoes than these?"

"I left a few pairs back in Washington. These are all I need except for my zoris."

"Well, we'll go shopping tomorrow. I'll take the day off and we can have lunch. Would you like that, Izzy?"

"Sure," I said, a big smile on my face. "I'd like that."

"Well, is there anything else you need now?" she asked me.

"I was thinking I'd put my books on one of the shelves," I told her. "Is that okay?"

"Of course it is. Here, let me take away this big box of pictures."

"Are they family pictures?" I asked her.

"Uh-huh." She was carrying them out of the room but she stopped. "Would you like to see them?"

"Well, sure," I said. "Sure."

"I'll bring them into the living room. It might be fun for all of us to look at them. I know you and your parents are in some of the old ones. Finish your unpacking, Izzy, and I'll make breakfast and then we can look at the photos. Oh

—and what do you generally eat for breakfast, by the way?"

"Anything is fine," I told her.

"But what do you like?"

"I eat everything."

She shook her head. "How about some eggs?"

"Well, if you and Uncle Roger eat eggs . . ."

"Izzy, I'm asking you if you like eggs. Never mind what we like," she said kind of quickly. Then she took a breath, smiled, and said much more slowly, "We generally have a croissant or an English muffin but if you like eggs, Izzy, I'll be happy to make some."

"I like croissants and English muffins," I told her.

"Orange juice? Milk?"

"Well sure if you have them."

She walked out of the room and I finished putting all my things away. I put Sandy's two candles on the chest right below the pigeon-dropping painting but they didn't look right there so I stuck them on one of the shelves in the closet. I put my two suitcases into the closet and after I'd made the bed, the room looked just the way it had before I arrived.

My uncle was sitting on the couch, still in his bathrobe, with the Sunday paper in front of him. My father always got dressed in the mornings which is why I always got dressed too. But if my aunt and uncle sat around in their bathrobes on the weekends I supposed I'd better learn to do the same.

"Good morning, Izzy," my uncle said, looking up.

"Good morning, Uncle Roger."

Both of us smiled and waited.

"How did you sleep?" my uncle asked.

"Oh, just fine."

"Was the bed comfortable?"

"Oh yes."

"Do you have everything you need?"

"Oh yes."

We continued smiling and I could see he was thinking of what to say next. So was I. Luckily, Aunt Alice came into the room then to say that breakfast was ready.

We ate in the kitchen, a white-and-black-tiled room with a glass table and white metal chairs. It was tough going. They asked me a lot of questions and I tried to answer the way I thought they would want me to answer.

"Do you have a lot of friends in Washington?" my aunt asked.

"Oh no," I told her. "I hardly ever brought friends over to my house. Mrs. Evans always said I was the quietest child she knew and the least messy."

"But didn't you have any friends at all?" They both were looking at me, not even chewing their croissants or sipping their coffee. I guess that hadn't been the right answer so I said cheerfully, "Oh, I had friends in school but I never brought them home. Sometimes Linda Altman—she lived downstairs—sometimes she came upstairs and we watched TV together. But we never made a mess."

I didn't ask them any questions at breakfast because I knew that most grown-ups don't like kids to ask questions. But later, when Aunt Alice and I were sitting around the table looking at pictures, I did ask questions like "Who was that?" and "How old were you when this was taken?"

There were lots of pictures and she seemed to enjoy looking at them as much as I did. I always liked looking at
photographs. We didn't have very many at home. My
father never took pictures and the ones I took weren't
always clear.

Photographs made me happy. Seeing people in bathing
suits on the beach or standing, all dressed up, in front of
some famous building on a trip, I liked to make believe I
was there too, making donkey fingers behind some kid's
head or singing in a chorus with a whole bunch of girls all
dressed in white dresses.

"Is that you?" I asked Aunt Alice, picking one out from
about thirty faces.

"No, no, Izzy, I'm over here. The little fat one. Would
you believe I could have been such a blimp?" She pushed
the picture away and picked up another. "Here, Izzy, look
at this one. Here's your father and your Uncle Roger."

Two boys, leaning against each other and grinning at
the camera. The smaller one, my father, in a striped tee
shirt and shorts. He had a bandaid on one knee and a
bunch of teeth missing in his mouth. My father—a little
boy just grinning at the camera.

"Who took it?" I asked.

"What? Oh—the picture? Roger," my aunt called.
"Who took this picture of you and Mark?"

"Hmm?" My uncle tore himself away from his newspa-
per and came over to the table and picked up the picture.
He smiled and shook his head over it. "My father took it,
Izzy. Your grandfather."

He laughed. "We were supposed to go and visit my
Aunt Margaret—my father's sister—your great aunt, Izzy,

and my mother said we had to change our clothes but I guess my father must have liked the way we looked because he took the picture." Uncle Roger laughed a little, soft laugh. Then he looked at me. "Do you remember him, Izzy? He was still alive before you left?"

"No," I said. "I don't remember."

He seemed disappointed. "He was so happy when you were born. I remember he waited at the hospital with Mark and he took lots and lots of pictures of you when you were little."

"Where are they?" I asked, really excited. "Where are my pictures?"

Some of them were in the box. Pictures of me as a baby by myself, with my Uncle Roger and Aunt Alice, with my father and mother. There was a big one of just me and my mother—me, a tiny baby, and my mother with a big smile on her face. A pretty face. I didn't look anything like her.

"She was so pretty," my Aunt Alice murmured, "and she had such a happy laugh. Do you remember her, Izzy?"

"No," I said, looking hard at the picture.

My aunt let out her breath the way grown-ups do when they're thinking of something sad. "She was so proud of you. She spent a lot of money on all sorts of little dresses and your father—well, they were just starting out and he used to make believe he didn't approve but he was really just as bad. They were like two kids with a doll. Here, look at this one, Izzy. Here they both are with you."

Another photograph with both of them sitting on a couch and me, a little older, on my father's lap, laughing and reaching out like I wanted to grab the camera. My father was holding me and he wasn't looking at the camera. He was smiling at me and looking at me. Just at me. I didn't feel good when I saw his smile and I put the picture down and took some others out of the box.

"You don't remember your mother at all?" my uncle asked.

"No," I told him. "Who's this, Uncle Roger?"

"Oh—that's Aunt Alice and her brother when they were little."

"Well, she was only four when Sally died," said my aunt. "No wonder she doesn't remember."

"Who's this, Aunt Alice?"

I was beginning to feel bad, looking at all those family pictures, especially the ones of me with my parents. I couldn't remember my mother. Sometimes, when I tried, I could almost hear somebody laughing in another room but when I ran into that room, in my mind, it was always Sandy sitting there.

"My parents when they were little. And here's one of me in kindergarten."

I didn't want to look at pictures anymore but by now both of them were sitting with me at the table, kind of happy and excited at seeing all those old faces and remembering them.

"Here's my friend, Joey Carlson, Alice. Remember, I told you all about him. He was my buddy in high school and he always copied off me, especially in chemistry. And you know what, Izzy?"

"No, what?" I asked brightly.

"Today he's a famous astrophysicist down at Stanford and I like to think it's thanks to me."

He laughed and Aunt Alice laughed and so I laughed. Without thinking, I picked a picture out of the box, looked at it, and, suddenly, I felt happier than I had felt in a long, long time.

"Gus," I yelled. "It's Gus."

My aunt and uncle looked at the picture with me but neither of them said anything. It was a picture of a picnic. A bunch of people were sitting on the grass with picnic baskets around them. Somebody was eating a sandwich and somebody was drinking from a can of beer. My mother and father were talking to Aunt Alice, and Uncle Roger was sitting near two other people. He had one of those sudden smiles, like when you know somebody's trying to take a candid picture and you've caught him in the act. And there was a little girl, me, in shorts and a ruffly shirt, playing with a little black dog who was wagging his tail so furiously that the tail was blurred.

"Oh, it's Gus! It's Gus!" I said again.

"My God!" said my uncle. "I didn't even know we had a picture of that."

"Your father must have taken it," my aunt said to him very quickly. "He was the only one who had a camera that day."

I was so happy, I couldn't stop talking. "That was my dog. Gus. I loved Gus. We used to have so much fun. He slept in a little dog bed with a plaid-colored mat in the kitchen and every morning I'd get up before everybody else and go and play with him. And one night I woke up and I took Gus into bed with me but he barked and barked and my father woke up . . ."

They were both looking at me. Not saying anything.

Not smiling. Just watching me. Maybe they were disgusted the way I was jabbering on and on. So I stopped. But I was still feeling happy. I put the picture down but I didn't want to let it out of my hands. So I picked it up again and said to my uncle, "Can I have this picture, Uncle Roger? Please? I mean not to keep but just to look at for a while."

"Well, sure," he said. "Sure. And Izzy, if you want any others—with your parents—you can have them too."

"No, just this one. I just want this one. Thanks, Uncle Roger. Thanks, Aunt Alice. I'll be careful with it."

That afternoon, they took me all over San Francisco to see the sights. It was a long, draggy day where I had to keep smiling and saying ooh and ah. They showed me the view from Golden Gate Bridge and from the top of Coit Tower. They took me for a walk in Golden Gate Park and we drank tea in the Japanese Tea Garden. Aunt Alice told me about her two nephews. One was ten and the other was thirteen and both of them liked to climb the moon bridge in the Japanese Tea Garden. So I said I'd like to climb it too and the two of them stood and watched me and asked if I enjoyed it when I came down.

Gus's picture was waiting for me when we got home. I had put it in the top drawer of one of the chests in the guest room and I took it out and almost laughed out loud. Gus! It was Gus! He used to lick my face and once I licked his and it felt all wet and furry. I had forgotten about Gus but now it all came back to me and I could even remember the taste of his fur on my tongue. Gus!

4

Aunt Alice took off the next day to go shopping with me.

We climbed into her beige-colored car with its spotless white-and-beige seats and I wondered if I was going to end up all in whites and beiges as well.

"Now, Izzy, I want you to tell me what you need," she said as we drove downtown. "I'm a little out of practice. I only have Jeff and Danny, my nephews, so I don't really know what girls wear nowadays."

"Same kind of clothes," I told her. "Jeans, sweaters, shirts."

Which is what I was wearing that day.

She gave me a quick, worried look. "Well, for now, I suppose it won't matter so much. I'm afraid, Izzy, you'll have to go to the local public school to finish up the term. It's too late to get you into boarding school but it will only be until June and it is within walking distance."

"I went to a public school in Washington," I told her.

"You did?" she cried. "In Washington?"

"I liked it," I said, and then felt foolish. "I mean," I continued, trying to think of something I didn't like. "The lunches were yukky and Mr. Harrison, he was my teacher this term, he was always yelling at this boy, Freddie Bullock. Not at me, though. I've never had any trouble with my teachers. I always get along."

She waited a few seconds and then she said, looking straight ahead, "Your uncle and I, Izzy, we really understand what you're going through now. We know it can't be easy for you, being uprooted this way from your home, your school, your friends."

"It's okay," I told her.

"Please, Izzy," my aunt said quickly, "just let me finish. We want you to be happy, Izzy. You haven't had an easy time. We know that and we want you to think of us as your family and tell us what we can do to make you feel at home."

"I don't want to go to boarding school," I said right out. She said to tell her so I did but it was a mistake. I knew it as soon as I said it. Me and my big mouth.

She drew in her breath and took a couple of quick sniffs. "I'm afraid, Izzy . . . ," she began.

"It's okay," I told her. "It's okay."

"You see, Izzy, it's just that we can't. Both of us work. I travel a great deal and there would be nobody to really look after you."

"I'm used to it," I told her. "I'm used to looking after myself. Dad always said . . ."

"Yes, Izzy, I know. I have an idea what's been happening. But your uncle and I want you to have a happy, rich life full of friends and good times now. What all children should have. We're busy people, Izzy, and we decided not to have children when we were married because each of us wanted to devote all our time to our careers. It wouldn't be fair to have a child—the kind of people we are—busy all the time in our work."

"My father was busy all the time," I told her. "And Sandy made candles and sometimes I could be with her but lots of times when she was married to Dad she wasn't home. And Karen, well, she got pregnant right away and she was sick and I tried not to bother her. And after Jeremy was born, she and Dad split. So I'm used to it, Aunt Alice."

Aunt Alice pulled over to one side of the road and parked the car. Then she turned and looked at me. Very seriously. It's hard not to laugh when somebody looks at you out of such a serious face. "I'm very glad we're having this talk, Izzy. I always feel it's the best thing for everybody to be honest. I hope you agree."

"Oh, I do, I do," I said, trying to keep my face solemn.

"I think you're probably very mature for your age, Izzy, but you are only eleven and you do need supervision and guidance. You're far too young to have to worry about anything."

"I don't worry," I said smiling. "You don't have to worry about me worrying."

"Your father, Izzy," said my aunt with a look like she was smelling moldy cheese, "was a fine man."

"Yes," I agreed. "He was for the underdog."

"But I think he didn't understand that young girls need a lot of attention."

"We got along fine," I told her. "He said himself that I was good at not bothering him."

My aunt started up the car again. "Boarding school is fun, Izzy," said my aunt. "Lots of my friends went. I used to be so jealous when they came home at Christmas with all those wonderful stories about secret clubs they had and then those cute uniforms they always wore. You'll see, Izzy, you're really going to have a good time. And you make friends there you keep for a lifetime. My friend, Charlotte Halbrook, has a friend from Belgium whom she met in boarding school."

Maybe she was right, I thought, sinking back exhausted into my seat. I was tired of always having to smile and agree with everything she said. Maybe boarding school would be the best place for a person like me.

She spent a lot of money that day. To begin with, she bought me three new pairs of jeans, four shirts, and four matching sweaters. All of them had fancy labels on them and cost maybe three or four times as much as the ones I usually bought. Then she picked out a couple of preppy plaid skirts, some preppy blazers, two summer dresses, socks, pajamas, a bathrobe, and two pairs of shoes.

"We'll really get you some clothes after the summer," she said, kind of apologizing. "Before you go away to school. Although most schools require uniforms, you'll need some things for weekends and holidays."

We ate lunch quickly because my aunt wanted to register me in the local school. You could see she wasn't happy about the school even though the kids looked pretty much the same as the kids in Washington. Only the building looked different—smaller, cleaner, and with a red-tiled roof.

"It's only for a couple of months," my aunt kept saying.

Back home, I unpacked my new clothes and hung them up in the closet. I like new clothes. They always make me feel as if something new and better will happen to me. I took my picture of Gus out of the drawer and I felt so happy, I wanted to share some of that good feeling with my aunt. So I put on a new pair of jeans, a new yellow-plaid shirt and yellow sweater, and looked at myself in the mirror. Same old me, I thought, feeling just a little disappointed. But when I came into the kitchen, my aunt nodded at me and smiled. "You really look lovely, dear," she said. "You can always see the difference in something that's well made."

She cocked her head to one side and examined me. "You know, Izzy, I think you could stand a good haircut. When was the last time you had one?"

"A couple of months ago, I guess."

"Well, let's see if we can line a haircut up for you today." She looked at her watch. "It's just about four and your uncle doesn't get home until after six. Let's surprise him."

Uncle Roger didn't seem very surprised when he saw me and Aunt Alice had to keep asking him if he didn't notice any difference in me before he caught on.

We had a fancy chicken for dinner and the conversation picked up a little bit. But then my uncle asked me what I wanted to be when I grew up. And I knew. I mean before that I always used to say a lawyer because that's what my father was. Suddenly I knew what I wanted to be. And it wasn't a lawyer.

"I want to be a vet," I told him.

He nodded and smiled at me. "That's nice, Izzy."

And then I asked him. "Where's Gus, Uncle Roger? Do you know where Gus is?"

His face folded up. He stopped smiling. "Why do you want to know?" he asked.

"Roger!" my aunt said.

"Because he was my dog and I want to see him. If he's alive, I want to see him again. Do you know where he is?"

"Did your father tell you about Gus?" my uncle asked. I'd seen plenty of mean prosecuting attorneys on TV and right now my uncle sounded like one of the meanest.

"Tell me what?"

"Roger," said my aunt, "I'm sure she doesn't know."

"It's okay," I told them. "It's okay." I twirled my fork around in a mound of mashed potatoes and tried to look unconcerned.

I could feel my uncle watching me as I lifted my fork to my mouth and tried not to drop any of the potatoes. Finally, he said, "I'm sorry, Izzy. I didn't mean to jump at you like that."

"It's okay, Uncle Roger," I said. "I didn't get upset."

"Roger," my aunt said. "I think you should tell her."

"It's okay . . ." I began.

"And will you please stop saying it's okay, Izzy!"

I didn't say anything to her because the only thing I could think of saying was okay.

"You keep saying it all the time," my aunt said, "and you don't mean it so please stop saying it."

"I don't know why you're jumping on her," said my uncle. "She didn't do anything to deserve it."

"Well, you're the one who started it," said my aunt, standing up. "And now you're turning on me."

"Alice," my uncle said, "you're blowing up over nothing."

"I'm sorry," I said.

"For what?" my aunt shouted. "What are *you* sorry for?"

Then the two of them began fighting which made me a lot more comfortable. I always knew what was expected of me when my father and one of his wives fought. I picked up my plate and moved off to the kitchen. The two of them were really yelling now. So I scraped off my dishes, loaded them into the dishwasher, and tiptoed into the guest room. This time, I closed the door.

After a while, my uncle knocked on the door. "May I come in, Izzy?" he asked.

I opened the door and my uncle walked in. His face was still flushed but his voice was calm and polite as usual.

"Your aunt thinks I should tell you what happened to Gus. It's not a nice story," he said, looking at me nervously, "so if you'd rather, we can wait until you're ready."

"I'm ready now," I told him. "I really want to see Gus."

He looked over his shoulder but Aunt Alice wasn't in sight. I could hear the sound of dishes clattering in the kitchen.

"Izzy," he said, in a low voice, "are you sure your father didn't say anything to you about Gus?"

"No," I said, "he never did. But if you really don't want to talk about it, it's okay."

My uncle smiled and sat down on my bed. "That's one word you'd better stop using around here," he said.

"I'll try," I told him, smiling back. Then I sat down next to him and waited.

"Well, Izzy, it's not a nice story and I'm not going to try to defend myself or . . . ," he hesitated, ". . . your father. People often act unreasonably during crisis, and I'm afraid that's what happened."

I waited.

He nodded his head a few times and then began. "That picture you found in the box, Izzy. It was taken maybe a half hour before your mother died."

I must have made a little surprised sound because he put his arm on my shoulder and left it there for a while.

"I don't remember how it got into the box. My father, your grandfather, must have taken it along with other pictures on that same roll, and somehow they found their way here. We were having a picnic that day on Mount Tamalpais. Your Aunt Alice and I were there, my father, our friends John and Bev Politi, your parents, you, and Gus. They'd only had Gus for six or seven months. Your mother found him one day, abandoned in the park, and took him home. She really enjoyed him and I guess you did too. But that day, at the picnic, it started getting cloudy and cold and we all began packing up to go home. Your mother called Gus but he was chasing after birds and she went running after him. The last thing we all heard was her calling him and laughing."

I sat very still and tried to remember my mother calling

Gus. But nothing happened. Inside my head, it stayed dark and still. My uncle patted my shoulder and went on.

"It was a freak thing—a once-in-a-million kind of accident. She was running after him up a little rocky hill and she tripped on something and fell over the hill. When we got to her, she was dying. She had broken her neck—a crazy, crazy accident. In a few minutes, she was dead."

"But Gus?" I said. "What happened to Gus?"

"Yes, well, that's another terrible thing. Izzy, are you sure you want to hear?"

I nodded and he took his arm off my shoulder, put both hands in his lap, and kept looking at them.

"I think now I made the wrong decision. If I had to do it over again, maybe I would have let him have his way. Maybe not. I wanted to do what was best for him. Really, Izzy, that's what I really wanted. Because he wasn't himself when she died. He went crazy. Of course, he always did have a temper."

"Yes," I said. "I know."

"Not that he ever hurt anyone."

"No," I said. "He never hurt anyone."

"But I'd never seen him like that. He was screaming and the little dog was frightened and Mark ran after it with a rock in his hand, yelling and screaming with the tears running down his face."

Now there was something moving inside the darkness in my head. Something terrible. Something that made me put my hands up to my ears. But I could still hear myself saying, "He tried to kill Gus."

My uncle's sad face watched me and I put my hands down and listened.

"He did but I went after him and I held him until the others came. My father and John, they had to help me—he was like a wild man. Then the ambulance came and they gave him a shot to quiet him down and took him away with her—with your mother. Your grandfather went with him."

"But Gus? What happened to Gus?"

"You see, Izzy, that's what I did wrong. I'd forgotten about Gus but just as your aunt and I were leaving with you—we had you with us that night, Izzy. I guess you don't remember?"

"No," I said, "I don't remember."

"We were just about ready to get into our car when the little dog, Gus, came running out of the bushes where he'd been hiding, and came over to us. I should have left him there."

"Oh no," I said. "No."

"I should have, Izzy. Somebody would have found him. He was such a cute little dog. But he began whining and he was trembling. Aunt Alice said I should leave him but he was crying like a little baby."

"You didn't leave him!"

"No, I didn't leave him. You started crying too. You said you wanted him so I took him back with us to the city and I gave him to—I gave him to a person I knew liked animals—but later, when your father asked me where Gus was, I didn't tell him. I should have told him. Maybe if he asked me again, I would have. Maybe not. Two weeks after she died, he took you and left town and never spoke to me again. My father—your grandfather—died that same year. I think if he had lived longer, Mark and I might have been able to work it out. I tried. I did, Izzy, I wrote to him but he always sent my letters back unopened."

"Where is Gus, Uncle Roger?" I asked him.

He looked at me and again his face hardened. "Izzy," he said, "if you're still thinking revenge after all these years . . ."

"You don't understand, Uncle Roger. I love Gus. I mean, I loved him. And he loved me. He was my dog. I don't want to hurt him. I want to see him. Just tell me where he is!"

5

He told me.

There was a woman, kind of a nutty woman, who hated people and loved animals. She was an old woman and she had been an old woman for as long as my uncle could remember. Her name was Mrs. Firestone even though, he said, nobody could ever remember a Mr. Firestone. When my uncle and my father were little boys they had lived in a house next to hers. Everybody in the neighborhood always complained about her because she had so many animals and her house was so run-down.

"She was the only one I could think of, so on the way back that day, I stopped at her house. She was just the same as ever. Her house stank of cats and dogs and God knows what else," said my uncle.

"You gave her Gus?" I cried.

"Yes, Izzy, I did. You were asleep and when you woke

up and asked for him I suppose we must have made up
some kind of story. When you went back to your father, I
don't know what he told you." He looked at me and
waited.

"I don't know either. I don't remember."

My uncle cleared his throat. "Sometimes I think he—
Mark—your father—must have known where the dog
was. Sometimes I think he really didn't want to hurt it.
Maybe just for a little while, when she died, he did. But
after, I don't think he really ever tried to find it. I just wish
. . . ." My uncle never said what it was he wished. I asked
him. "Is she still there?"

"Who?"

"The lady with the animals. Mrs. Firestone."

"I don't know," he said. "It was seven years ago. She was
an old lady."

"Please, Uncle Roger," I begged. "Call her up. Call her
up now."

He shook his head. "I'm sorry, Izzy, but she was always a
very eccentric lady and she never had a phone."

"Where does she live?"

"On Mimosa Street. We used to live there—126 Mimosa
—and she lived right next door."

"Please, Uncle Roger, can we go there now? Please?"

"I tell you what, Izzy," he said, "maybe on Saturday we
can take a drive over there and see if Mrs. Firestone is still
there. Maybe you'd like to see 126 where we lived for so
long. I haven't been over there for years. Your father and I
had a tree house in the backyard and my mother had two
beautiful rhododendron bushes that just might be in
bloom now. She was so proud of those bushes."

"But Uncle Roger that's a whole week away."

"I'm sorry, Izzy, but I have a very busy schedule this week." He looked at his watch. "Tomorrow, I'm meeting some clients and I need to look over a bunch of papers tonight. The rest of the week I'm going to be up to my ears in meetings and conferences. But Saturday I'll take you, Izzy. I promise. Is that all right?"

It wasn't but I didn't tell him.

"Sure, Uncle Roger," I said.

Aunt Alice walked me to school the next morning. She gave me a key to the apartment and my lunch money and stood in the school yard with a worried look. "Now remember, Izzy, Gina, the young woman who cleans for me, will be at home when you get back. I've arranged for her to work afternoons instead of mornings as long as you're with us. So she'll be there when you get home today. You're sure you don't want her to pick you up at school?"

"Aunt Alice," I said, "I'm eleven years old and the apartment is only three blocks away."

"But just for this first time?"

"I'll be fine, Aunt Alice."

She nodded, her face still worried. "And you do know how to get to the principal's office? Somebody there will take you to your classroom. Maybe I ought to come with you."

"Oh no, Aunt Alice," I said. "I know where the office is."

Aunt Alice smiled. "I guess you don't want anybody to think you're a baby," she said. "I guess it would embarrass you."

"That's right," I told her. "It would embarrass me."

"Well." She looked around the yard at the kids running and shouting and laughing. "Well." She lowered her voice. "I don't think this school has too bad a reputation, but Izzy, if anybody bothers or upsets you . . ."

"Oh, they won't," I said, eager for her to go.

Two girls hurried by, dressed in jeans, shirts, and sweaters like mine but without the fancy labels. She watched them doubtfully. "Would you want to call me at lunch?" she asked.

"I don't know where the phone is," I said. "Please don't worry, Aunt Alice. I'll be fine."

She was trying hard, and she smiled a brave smile. "No, of course not, Izzy. Well, I'll be going now. I won't kiss you good-bye because I don't want to embarrass you. Have a good day, dear."

"Oh, I will. I will," I told her.

I moved into the building and waited. I began counting —one, two, three. . . . Groups of kids passed me as they ran up the stairs . . . thirty-five, thirty-six. . . . Two boys clowning around bumped into me . . . sixty-nine, seventy. . . . A mother ran after a girl, calling, "Rachel, Rachel, you left your lunch. You'd forget your head if it wasn't on your shoulders" . . . one hundred eleven . . . one hundred twelve . . .

When I counted up to three hundred, I stepped outside and looked carefully around. My aunt was nowhere in sight. So slowly, very slowly, I walked out of the school yard and down the street in the opposite direction to the apartment. I was not going to school that day. I was going to see Gus. I couldn't wait until Saturday.

In a service station, they told me which buses to take to

Mimosa Street. I had a story all ready in case anybody wanted to know why I wasn't in school. I was going to tell them that my family had just moved to 126 Mimosa that morning and that I was supposed to pick up some books at school and then hook up with my older brother, Jeremy, who was eighteen and was going to drive me over where we would join our parents and baby sister, Rachel. But Jeremy must have gotten mixed up because he wasn't there when I picked up my books and the phone wasn't installed yet at 126 Mimosa and I knew my mother would worry if I didn't get there as soon as possible.

Nobody asked me. There were two men and a teenage boy at the service station and all three of them got into an argument as to the best way to go. It wasn't a very big street and they had to look for it on a map which kept them too busy to think about me. Which was great.

I sat on the first bus and looked out the window and thought about Gus. I knew he was alive. He had to be alive. He would be between seven and eight years old. Not so old for a dog. Somebody said each dog year is like seven years for a person. Seven times seven makes forty-nine. Eight times seven makes fifty-six. I didn't believe Gus could be forty-nine or fifty-six. Dogs live until they are fifteen or sixteen. I couldn't multiply double numbers in my head but I figured it would be over one hundred, and I didn't want to think about Gus being over one hundred, dred.

I had to transfer to another bus and a friendly lady with two packages sat down next to me. I was sure she was going to ask me why I wasn't in school but she didn't. She dropped her keys and I picked them up for her. Then she

asked me if I'd like a mint. When I said no, she asked me to
hold her packages while she looked in her bag for the
mints. Then she told me her daughter lived in New York
and her son was in college. She forgot to take the packages
back and I didn't want to interrupt her while she was
talking. I was afraid she might remember to ask me why I
wasn't in school.

I kept watching for Mimosa but some of the street signs
were missing and often the bus went whizzing by the
corners too fast for me to read them anyway. This part of
the city wasn't as new and glamorous as the part my uncle
and aunt lived in. The people on the streets looked poorer
and I didn't suppose there would be any fancy labels on
their clothes.

The lady was telling me about her husband's old car. It
was all banged up and she was afraid to drive around in it
herself which was one of the reasons she took the bus.

"Excuse me," I interrupted, as politely as possible. "Are
we coming to Mimosa?"

She said I should get off at the stop after the next one.
She took her packages back and I buzzed the buzzer and
wiggled by her.

"Nice talking," she said to me.

Mimosa was a funny, old, twisty street that began climb-
ing as soon as I stepped off the bus. The houses were old
and some of them looked shabby. I watched as the numbers climbed higher and higher along with the street and
I began wondering. What if Mrs. Firestone wasn't there?

I couldn't work that out in my mind but I guess all along
I knew she would be there. Some old ladies never die and
I knew she would be one of them.

The rhododendron bushes were blooming in front of 126 Mimosa but I didn't stop. Right next door lived Mrs. Firestone and there she was, out in the messiest yard I'd ever seen, burning something that smelled like banana peels and old tennis shoes. There were cans and papers and bits of broken things lying all around her. Two rusty bikes stood propped up against a spindly eucalyptus tree and a rickety baby carriage without a baby in it leaned against one side of a small, crooked house set all the way in the back of the yard.

I heard barking, very faintly, coming from inside the house. Outside, a large, scruffy dog silently stood near his mistress and blinked at me as I came to a stop outside the gate.

In all my life I had never seen so many cats—here and there and everywhere, stretched out on the stairs, perched on the gate, prowling the yard—more cats than I could possibly count. And there were geese—two of them, waddling around in front of a child's plastic pool of water. But what I cared about most, what made my heart thump so hard up in my neck, was that faint barking coming from inside the house. Gus?

But first I had to make friends with Mrs. Firestone. She was stirring the fire with what looked like a long metal spoon, and she raised her head as I stood leaning on her gate, and narrowed her eyes inside of a face crumpled with wrinkles. I gave her the friendliest smile I could manage.

"Go away!" she said, waving her spoon at me. "Go away!"

"Mrs. Firestone," I said quickly, "my name is Isabelle Cummings."

She looked like a wicked old witch with the smoking fire beside her and the mean-looking cats, suddenly still, watching me.

"I know what you're up to," she said, shaking the spoon furiously. "Your mother sent you. You tell her I'm on to her."

"No, no, Mrs. Firestone," I told her. "I don't have a mother. You're mixing me up with someone else. My mother is dead."

"Your father, then," said Mrs. Firestone. "You can't fool me. I've seen you sneaking around and spying on me. You'd better be off now or I'll set Loretta on you." The big gray dog stiffened and snarled softly. From the house, I could still hear the faint barking.

"Please, Mrs. Firestone," I said quickly. "I'm not spying on you. My father's dead too. He used to live next door when he was a little boy. It's my uncle, Roger Cummings, he told me. He gave you a dog—Gus. He was my dog. It was seven years ago. I just wanted to come and see him."

"Gus?" Mrs. Firestone said. She stopped waving the spoon and slowly raised her head up and down, looking me over.

"Yes, Mrs. Firestone. I just wanted to come and see Gus. Please? May I see him? He was my dog and I loved him."

"Yes." Mrs. Firestone smiled. "Your uncle gave me a dog. I remember. About ten years ago, it was."

I knew it was seven but I didn't correct her. I just stood there, nodding politely.

"A nice dog," Mrs. Firestone said. "But I don't call him

Gus. I call him Spencer. All my animals I call after famous actors and actresses. Except for the geese."

"Can I see him, Mrs. Firestone? Could you call him please?"

"Oh, but he never comes outside anymore. He catches cold very easily. Today is so mild though that I said to him, 'Spencer, I think you can take a chance today. It's a lovely day, so warm and sunny. Just come out for a little while.' But you can't budge him when he makes up his mind. And just listen to him. He's been like that all morning and I can't imagine why he's so worked up."

She stopped talking and we both listened to the dog inside the house barking and barking. Was it because he knew I had come? My Gus! Even though she called him Spencer, he had not forgotten me.

"Can I . . . ?" I began and stopped but she knew what I wanted.

"Certainly," she said, smiling and showing a perfectly even set of false teeth that didn't match her crooked, wrinkled face. "Come right in. Spencer will be delighted to see you."

I walked into the yard and she reached for my arm and led me to the house at the back. She smelled old and dry like old newspapers but I didn't mind. Inside, the house was crowded with piles of furniture, magazines, and old stacks of carpets. You could smell cats everywhere. I could hear Gus barking but I still didn't see him.

"Turn left, dear. He's in the kitchen," said Mrs. Firestone, hanging on to my arm. "He likes the kitchen. Now that he's so old, he likes to be near his food." She chuckled.

"That's all he's really interested in these days is his food—silly old dog."

"But he's not so old," I cried. "He's only seven or eight. That's not so old for a dog."

"Oh, he's older than that," said Mrs. Firestone, her fingers tightening on my arm. "He was old when I got him. He's the oldest one in this house. He's even older than me."

She pushed me through a small, dark hall into an even darker kitchen that smelled of old fish.

"You've got company today, Spencer," said Mrs. Firestone.

He was on a blanket under an ancient stove and when he saw me enter the room, he stood up and his bark turned into a whine.

"You can pet him, dear," said Mrs. Firestone. "Even if he wanted to bite you, he couldn't. He only has a few teeth left."

I didn't want to pet him because the old white dog watching me wasn't Gus.

"That's not Gus," I cried.

"No, it's Spencer," said Mrs. Firestone. "I told you his name was Spencer."

The dog began barking again. "No, no, Mrs. Firestone," I said. "Gus, my Gus was a little black dog. Not a white one."

"Now stop it, Spencer." The old lady let go of my arm and moved over toward the dog. She patted his head and he stopped barking and licked her hand. "Go ahead, dear," she said to me. "You can pet him if you like."

I shook my head and tried not to cry. "He's not my dog.

Please, Mrs. Firestone. My uncle said he brought you my dog, Gus, a little black dog. He said he left him here with you seven years ago."

"Oh that dog!" said Mrs. Firestone. She opened the refrigerator and took out a plate with a powerful, fishy smell and set it down in front of the dog.

"He likes sardines," she said, "mashed. He and the cats —they all like sardines. But Rudolph, my other dog, he prefers Italian salami."

"What happened to Gus?"

She took my arm and led me outside the house again. The fire was roaring up even higher and smellier and a very angry-looking woman with a small boy was standing outside the gate.

"That dog," Mrs. Firestone said. "Loretta scared him."

"Loretta?"

"Loretta—over there—my cat, Loretta." A very large, heavy calico cat sat up on top of the gate, looking at me out of heavy, sleepy eyes.

"Loretta scared him. She was younger in those days and a lot meaner." Mrs. Firestone chuckled. "She's much more mellow now."

"Mrs. Firestone . . ." the angry-looking woman began.

"She chased him all over the place, poor little thing. He was only a puppy, and so cute. But he cried all the time. I guess he missed the people he used to live with, and Loretta wouldn't leave him alone."

"Mrs. Firestone, I am going to call the police unless you put out that fire this instant," said the woman.

Mrs. Firestone acted as if she had not heard a word.

"She scratched him up too. I tried to reason with her but she wouldn't listen. She always had a mind of her own."

". . . a disgrace to the neighborhood," said the woman. "I've warned you over and over again and I know the health department . . ."

"So I had to give him away. I didn't want him to be unhappy, poor little thing."

"But who did you give him to, Mrs. Firestone? Do you remember who you gave him to?"

". . . unless you put that fire out this second!"

"Of course I remember who *I* gave him to," said Mrs. Firestone. "I called the S.P.C.A., and as for you, Madam, unless you get away from that gate this minute, I'll set my cat on you!"

6

All the way home I thought about Gus. I thought about how he and I used to roll around on the floor together, me holding on to him, over and over and over again. He liked me the best, I knew that. He even liked me better than he did my mother.

Not that I could remember her but I could remember that he liked me the best. Why should anybody blame him for my mother's death? Hadn't my uncle called it a freak accident—a once-in-a-million kind of accident? My father didn't know what he was doing. I put my hands over my ears and made myself stop thinking about my father. I only wanted to think about Gus, about finding him again and making it up to him.

But maybe he's happy now, I thought as I let myself into the apartment. Maybe the S.P.C.A. found a wonderful family with a girl like me and they're all crazy about Gus. It was funny but even though I tried my best to feel good for Gus I couldn't help being jealous of that girl who was just my age and who Gus loved as much as he had once loved me.

No, not as much, I thought. But if he's happy with her and if she's good to him, I suppose I can learn to accept it. I picked up the phone in the guest room, dialed 411 and asked Information for the number of the S.P.C.A. It rang for a long time before a man picked it up. I could hear dogs barking behind him.

"Hello," I said. "I'd like some information on a dog who was brought in about seven years ago. His name was . . ."

"What?" he said.

". . . Gus. His name was Gus and I'd like to know what happened to him."

"No, no, no!" the man yelled but not at me. "Wait a minute. You're hurting him." I could hear a dog howling. "Now, what was that?" he said again to me.

"Uh . . . I was wondering . . ."

"Look," said the man, "we've got an emergency here. Let me transfer your call."

"Well, but . . ." The line went dead for a moment or two and then another man picked up the phone and said, "Hello."

"Hello," I said quickly, "I wonder if I could get some information."

"Certainly," he said, politely. "What would you like to know?"

I took a deep breath. "About seven years ago, a little dog named Gus was given to the S.P.C.A. by a lady named Mrs. Firestone. He was my dog. I mean, I was only four years old then so it wasn't my idea to give him away. But

anyway, I was wondering if you could please tell me
where he is. I moved away and now I'm back and I want to
see him again."

Just as he began to answer, I heard the outside door to
the apartment open.

"I'm very sorry," the man was saying, "but that's not
possible."

I heard footsteps crossing the living room, coming
down the hall, and a young woman stuck her head in the
doorway and smiled at me. The cleaning woman! I'd forgotten about the cleaning woman.

"Hello?" said the man on the phone. "Hello?"

"Uh—hello."

The young woman nodded and moved away.

"Did you hear what I just said?"

"Yes, I did," I said, lowering my voice, "but I don't
understand why you can't tell me."

"We consider that kind of information confidential," he
said. "Once a dog is placed in a new home it is not in his
best interests to see his old owners."

"But I just want to see if he's happy," I said. "I'm not
going to make trouble or bother anyone."

"I'm sure he's happy," said the man. "We only put our
animals into homes where we feel people will take good
care of them."

A wonderful idea came to me.

"Well, why couldn't you just tell them about me? About
how I'd like to know how he is. Maybe they could call me
and tell me or write to me."

I felt certain that once Gus's new owners contacted me,
they could be persuaded to let me come and see him.

Even the girl, the one he loved nearly as much as me, even she could be persuaded.

The man hesitated.

"Please," I said. "It's very important to me. Something terrible happened. My mother died and I was too little to . . . to stop it. We moved away and . . . Gus was given away . . . please!"

"I'm sorry," said the man. "I'd really like to help you. . . ."

"Please!"

"How long ago did you say the dog was brought in?"

"Seven years ago. His name is Gus. He's a little black dog—a mutt, I guess, and the lady's name who gave him up was Mrs. Firestone."

"In a few months," the man said, "all our records will be computerized but now it's very, very difficult to find anything especially that long ago."

"Please!" I guess my voice cracked and the man took a deep breath and said in a very cranky voice, "We're very short-staffed right now. We don't have enough people to take care of our present situation."

"Please!"

"And it would take weeks even if we could find somebody to look."

"I'll come," I said. "I can look. I can start today."

"Impossible!" he said, but he didn't sound so mean anymore. "I'm not promising but if you give me his number I'll see what I can do. Just remember, even if we do find him, I'd have to contact his owners first and see if they would agree."

"Oh yes," I said, "but why can't I help you look? It's such a long time to wait."

"What is the dog's number?" said the man.

"Number?"

"Yes. When an animal is brought in, we assign him a number."

"But his name is Gus."

"All our records are kept under the animal's number. The old owner has the number as well as the new."

"I don't have it," I cried.

"Then I'm afraid we can't help you," the man said gently. "There is no way we can locate an animal unless you have that number."

I couldn't think of anything to say. Not even okay.

"Hello?" said the man.

"Hello."

"You know we have some wonderful animals right now looking for a home—a beautiful little Siamese kitten and a very friendly German shepherd dog."

"No," I told him. "I just want Gus."

"I'm sorry," he said.

I could hear the cleaning woman rattling around outside the room and I tried to think of something to say to her. But my mind was on Gus. All I could think of was Gus.

She must have been listening for me to hang up because she stuck her head back into the room again and said, "Hi —I'm Gina. I know you're Izzy but your aunt said you wouldn't be home until three."

"Well . . . ," I said, "well . . ."

"I guess she thought you were eating lunch in school."

"Well," I said, "yes, I . . . I changed my mind."

Gina made a face. She was young and looked a lot like
Sandy. "I never could stand school lunches either. Do you
want me to make a sandwich for you?"

"Oh no," I said. "I can make my own."

"Do you know where everything is?"

"Not exactly, but . . ."

Gina showed me around the kitchen and talked non-
stop all the time I was eating my lunch. She was a college
student working her way through school but most of her
classes were night classes except for one at four in the
afternoon and she actually preferred not working mornings except for that one day when she had the four o'clock
class. She was planning to go into marine biology and her
boyfriend's name was Doug but he was interested in art
history. She didn't ask me anything about myself which
was lucky for me and I didn't really need to ask her anything to keep her talking. But I did ask her one question.

"Do you have a dog?"

"No, I don't like dogs. They're too mushy. I've got a cat
named Felix—a big, independent tiger. He goes his way
and I go mine."

When I was ready to leave, she said she would be waiting for me at three.

"I might be a little late," I told her. "I might—uh—want
to pick up a few books in the school library."

"Well, I'll be here," she said, and asked me to take the
garbage out on my way down.

It's always a good time to think when somebody's talking on and on and you're only half listening. All I had to do
was eat my sandwich, smile, and nod at Gina while she
was talking and say, "Oh?" or "No kidding" from time to

time. It came to me, while she was describing her boyfriend, I guess, so I'm not sure if she said his eyes were
gray and his hair brown or his eyes were brown and his
hair gray that if I had the number I would be able to find
my way to Gus. All I needed was the number, and grown-
ups, I knew, even weird ones like Mrs. Firestone, always
liked holding on to numbers.

I was getting used to taking buses in San Francisco.
Nobody asked me why I wasn't in school and I knew
where to get off when we reached Mimosa. As I climbed
up the street, I noticed this time that there were other
rhododendron bushes blooming in front of other people's
houses. Some were white and some were pink and some
had dark purple spots. I slowed down as I came to Mrs.
Firestone's house. I knew she had the number. She had to
have that number. I was in a great hurry to get that number and to find Gus but as I passed Number 126 my shoes
felt as if they had lead in them.

Slowly, very slowly, I leaned on the old, crooked gate
and looked into the yard. No rhododendron bushes
bloomed in Mrs. Firestone's yard. Only a few cats circled
the spot where the fire had burned that morning. Mrs.
Firestone was not in sight. Slowly, I opened the gate,
walked down the yard to the crooked house at the end, up
the crooked steps, and knocked at the door.

"Go away!" somebody shouted from inside.

I breathed a sigh of relief. Mrs. Firestone was at home.

"Mrs. Firestone," I called out. "It's me, Isabelle Cummings. I'm the girl who came this morning, looking for my
dog, Gus. You remember Gus, Mrs. Firestone, the little
black dog my uncle gave you seven years ago."

The door opened and Mrs. Firestone stood there, smiling.

"How nice to see you again," she said in a very ladylike manner. "Have you come back to see Spencer?"

"No, Mrs. Firestone, not Spencer. I'm still trying to find my dog, Gus. You remember, Mrs. Firestone. Loretta scared him and you gave him to the S.P.C.A."

Mrs. Firestone shook her head. "Poor little thing. Loretta scratched his nose and chased him under the bed. I told her to stop it. I . . ."

"Mrs. Firestone," I interrupted. "I need the number the S.P.C.A. gave you when they took Gus."

Mrs. Firestone's eyes were so pale it was hard to know what color they were. And her eyelashes were as white as her hair. She looked at me but didn't answer.

"The number the S.P.C.A. gave you, Mrs. Firestone. I called them and they said that whenever a dog is brought in they give it a number and that the old owner has the number as well as the new owner."

Mrs. Firestone shook her old head.

"They said they gave you the number, Mrs. Firestone. You have to find the number."

"I don't remember a number," said Mrs. Firestone. "It was so long ago."

"I'm sure you have it," I cooed at her. "Maybe I could help you find it."

"Do come in," said Mrs. Firestone, opening her door.

I followed her into the living room this time and both of us sat down on a filthy, torn couch and looked at each other. There were boxes and boxes stacked up on top of one another lining all the walls. I tried not to look at them.

"Maybe you put it away in your desk," I suggested, looking around the room for a desk.

The large gray dog who had snarled at me in the yard padded over and sniffed my knees.

"His name is Rudolph—after Rudolph Valentino," said Mrs. Firestone.

The dog sniffed both of my knees thoroughly and then, suddenly, he licked my hand.

"There, you see," Mrs. Firestone said. "He likes you. He knows you like animals. He's a very good judge of character."

I patted Rudolph's head. It felt good and I wondered if he had known Gus, if he had been there at the same time as my dog.

"How old is Rudolph?" I asked, scratching behind one of his ears.

"I don't remember," said Mrs. Firestone.

"Do you think he was here when Gus came here? Do you think they might have known each other?"

"It's possible," Mrs. Firestone admitted. "Would you like a cup of tea? And what is your name, my dear?"

"Isabelle but people call me Izzy." Rudolph rested his head on my knees and looked up at me.

"Would you like a cup of tea, Izzy?"

"No, thank you, but I do need to find that number, Mrs. Firestone. Do you have any idea where it might be?"

A small black-and-white cat jumped up on the sofa and began rubbing herself against me.

"That's Norma," said Mrs. Firestone. "She's named after Norma Shearer who was a beautiful actress. And there's her brother, Clark, that black cat with the white paws. He's named after Clark Gable."

"How many cats do you have, Mrs. Firestone?"

"It's hard to say. I never count."

The cat continued rubbing herself against me. I didn't mind even though I like dogs better.

"I need that number, Mrs. Firestone," I tried again.

"What number, Izzy?"

"Gus's number. The one the S.P.C.A. gave you."

"I don't know where it is."

"It was on a paper, Mrs. Firestone. Maybe you put it in your desk or maybe in one of those boxes or maybe in a drawer?"

Mrs. Firestone slowly began looking around the room. Norma stopped rubbing against me and settled down in her lap. Then her brother, Clark, jumped up on the couch and plopped down in her lap too. She began stroking his head and his eyes opened and closed as her wrinkled old hand moved back and forth. "I don't know," she said. "Sometimes I burn papers. Especially ones with numbers on them."

Rudolph raised his head from my knees and moved over to Mrs. Firestone. He laid his head on her lap, right next to Norma's face and the two animals looked sleepily into each other's eyes. The room was quiet but my despair pounded so noisily inside my chest that I could not keep it there. "I'll never find Gus now," I cried.

"Why not?" Mrs. Firestone asked in her dry old voice.

"Because the S.P.C.A. can't find out where he is unless

they have his number. I'll never know who they gave him to."

"But I know who they gave him to," said Mrs. Firestone. "Why didn't you ask?"

7

My father used to say if you want the right answers, you have to know how to ask the right questions. Looking back, I realized that I had not asked the right question which was "Where is Gus now?"

"They came and took him away, poor little thing," said Mrs. Firestone. "I think I cried the whole day. You know, Izzy," she said, putting her pale old face up close to mine. There were white wispy hairs on her chin and I tried not to look at them. "Sometimes they kill them—the S.P.C.A. does. I never like to give an animal away but he wasn't happy here."

"Where is he now, Mrs. Firestone?"

"Sometimes," Mrs. Firestone continued gloomily, ignoring my question, "they say they put them to sleep but I know they kill them. So I felt bad all day. But then, later, when I was shopping, the grocery man, Mr. Holland, was telling a customer that his dog had died. I never liked his dog. He always used to bark at me and once he chased my Rudolph down the street. The dog was a lot like Mr. Holland. But, of course, I was sorry he had passed on and I extended my sympathies to Mr. Holland. I also told him about Gus and do you know what happened?"

"He went to the S.P.C.A. and took Gus?"

"No, he wasn't interested but his customer was—a young woman with a little boy. She said she was looking for a dog. I told her Loretta had scared him and what a sweet, gentle dog he was. She said she wanted a gentle dog to play with her little boy and I said that Gus would be the perfect one. So she went and got him."

"Are you sure, Mrs. Firestone? Are you sure she went and got him?"

"Oh yes, because a couple of times I saw her in the store with him and once Mr. Holland told me that he had—you know what—all over the cans of tomatoes. So he asked her to keep him tied up outside."

Mrs. Firestone went on talking about other things but I was thinking about Gus. No girl like me for his owner but a boy. I preferred a boy. I wasn't going to be jealous of a boy.

"What kind of a boy was he?" I asked Mrs. Firestone.

"Who?"

"The boy who was with the lady who went and got Gus."

"Oh, that boy!"

"Was he a nice boy?"

"Well, Izzy," said Mrs. Firestone, "in general, I don't have a very high opinion of boys. Girls laugh at you and call you names but boys throw things." She lowered her voice. "You see my goose, Franklin—the one with the spotted neck? He's named for my favorite president, Franklin D. Roosevelt. I found him in the park. Ah, those were the days!" Mrs. Firestone had a faraway look in her eyes. "When I was younger, I used to take my baby carriage and go to the park and oh, the things I found! Watches and hats and umbrellas, toys and blankets and bottles of wine. Ah, those were the days!"

"You were telling me about the boy, Mrs. Firestone, the one who has Gus."

"Yes," said Mrs. Firestone, "so on that day, I saw them, three of them, three boys, throwing stones at Franklin here. They were running after him on the grass and he was hurt. So I hit one of them with my umbrella and I kicked another one and they ran away." She laughed a dry, high little laugh and her false teeth jiggled around in her mouth. "They called me names and threw stones at me but I'm used to that. Franklin was hurt. He had a cut on his back so I took him home with me in the baby carriage. I fixed him up but I could see he wasn't happy. So another day, I went back and took Eleanor home for him. Now he's happy."

"But that boy, Mrs. Firestone, the one with the lady. Did he look like a nice boy?"

Mrs. Firestone shrugged her shoulders. "He looked like a boy, a little boy."

"Did Gus seem happy?"

"Oh yes," she said. "He used to come right up to me whenever he saw me at the grocery store and he would wag his tail. Yes, I think he looked very happy."

"Do you know the lady's name?"

Mrs. Firestone shook her head. "No, and as a matter of fact I haven't seen her for a while. But Mr. Holland will know who she is. He didn't like the way the little dog used to—you know what—on his tomatoes."

Mrs. Firestone didn't want me to leave. She offered to show me a whole bunch of umbrellas she had found in the park. She said I could look them all over and even take one if I liked.

But she understood that I had to go. If anybody understood how much you could love an animal, it was Mrs. Firestone. She showed me the way to go to Mr. Holland's grocery store and said I should tell him that none of her animals had liked the last pound of butter he had sold her. "Too salty," she told me. "Next time, tell him, more butter and less salt."

The store was empty when I arrived. A large, round, bald man with more chins than I could count slouched over the counter and watched me carefully as I came toward him.

"Uh, Mrs. Firestone sent me over," I told him.

"Mrs. Firestone," said the grocer, straightening up and narrowing his eyes at me. "Mrs. Firestone now owes me three hundred dollars and seventy-eight cents. I don't know what she sent you over here for but maybe you'll be good enough to take a message back to her from me. The message is—*no more credit!*"

"Yes, sir," I said, and decided not to deliver Mrs. Firestone's message to him. "Actually, Mrs. Firestone didn't send me over here to buy anything. She sent me over here because she said you would be able to answer a question I have."

"Which is?" he asked, not very pleasantly.

So I went through the whole story about Gus and he shook his head when I finished.

"I don't know what she's talking about," he said. "I've been here for over thirty years and I've never known what she's ever been talking about."

"A lady with a little boy . . ."

"Lots of my customers are ladies with little boys."

"A small black dog . . ."

"And lots of them have small black dogs."

". . . named Gus."

"I don't listen to their names."

"Mrs. Firestone said he—you know what—on your cans of tomatoes."

"Oh that dog!" said Mr. Holland.

He remembered Gus. "Mrs. Kaplan. That was her name. Her husband was Dr. Kaplan, a young fellow doing an internship in one of the hospitals. Five, six years ago that was, but I remember because she always bought cans of okra. Her little boy was crazy about okra so I had to stock it just for her. You remember things like that when you're a grocer. I never had a customer before or one after who liked okra."

"But Mr. Holland, where is she now?"

He shrugged his shoulders. "Who knows? Once he finished interning, they moved and I was stuck with over a dozen cans of okra."

"Does anybody know where they moved, Mr. Holland?"

"But I don't hold it against her. She should have let me know in advance but I guess she didn't think of it. And she did come in to say good-bye. She was a good customer, so some things you just have to overlook."

"Please, Mr. Holland," I said, "I need to find them. Isn't there anybody who can tell me where they went?"

"Maybe," said Mr. Holland. "Maybe their old landlady, Mrs. Doyle. She rented them the upstairs apartment. She lives downstairs—148 Oleander—but she's probably not home now. You have to catch her in the mornings. In the afternoons she goes to baby-sit for her daughter."

I was aching with impatience but the clock in Mr. Holland's grocery store said ten to three. It would take me nearly an hour to get home and I didn't want Gina to grow suspicious. Tomorrow was another day.

We had crepes stuffed with shrimp and mushrooms and a big spinach and mandarin orange salad for dinner. And little chocolate tarts that my aunt pulled out of the freezer. I watched her working in her kitchen. Everything gleamed and nothing made stains or spots or splashes on the floor. Her beige skirt and off-white silk shirt stayed clean under the spotless white apron. She loved to cook, she told me as her long, slim fingers with their perfect nails quickly stirred, chopped, and cut. Often, on a free evening or Sunday, she said, she might cook or bake up a batch of things to freeze.

"Do you like to cook, Izzy," she asked me.

I hesitated. I thought of Mrs. Evans's meat loafs and spaghetti sauces and the rows of TV dinners in our freezer. Sandy never cooked much and Karen kept saying she would once she was over being pregnant. Sometimes

Mrs. Evans baked—big, lumpy marble cakes and cookies that were either too hard or too soft.

"Yes," I said, "yes, I like to cook."

"Well, maybe you and I can work together tonight if you like. Tomorrow night, I'm expecting some friends over. Some women. We have a women's reading group and we get together once a month at somebody else's house. Tomorrow night it's my turn, so I thought I might bake something tonight. Would you like to help?"

"Oh yes," I said. "I would."

"Unless," she said, "you have too much homework. I wouldn't want to interfere with your homework."

"Oh no," I told her. "I did it already."

They asked me a lot of questions about school at dinner. My aunt really asked me the questions and my uncle pretended to be interested in what I was saying. But I could see his mind was on other things. He was reminding me more and more of my father.

My aunt's face had such a serious, worried look as she asked her questions that I made a special effort to look bright and happy as I answered.

"What's your teacher's name?"

"Uh—Miss Ballard."

"Is she nice?"

"Oh yes. She's very nice. She's young and very pretty and the kids all seem to really like her."

"And the other children? The kids? Are they . . . are they nice?"

"Oh, just great! Very nice!"

"Are they . . . are they nice to you? I hope nobody said anything mean or . . ."

"Oh no. They went out of their way to help me. One of the girls showed me around the classroom and stayed with me during the day. And she picked me for her kickball team during PE. A great bunch of kids, Aunt Alice."

"Because you know, Izzy, if you're not happy there, I want you to let us know right away."

"I love it," I told her, smiling. "It's the best school I ever went to."

My uncle did the dishes but you could see he was in a big hurry to go off and look at his papers. Aunt Alice and I stayed in the kitchen and she began pulling out shiny baking pans and measuring spoons and gleaming mixing bowls.

"I thought we'd make a Gâteau Génoise for petits fours."

"Oh sure," I said.

"I don't know if you've ever made them before," she said, looking at me with that worried look.

"Well no, not exactly," I admitted, "but I'm a fast learner."

Later, she said I was. At first, she made me nervous, the way she worked, so clean and careful. But later, after she had baked a large pan of sweet, lemony-smelling cake and set it down in front of me to cut out shapes with different kinds of cookie cutters, I began to enjoy myself. I cut out squares and circles and diamonds and even some hearts. She gave me jams and creams and chocolate icing and nuts and fruits to fill them with and her face stopped looking so worried.

They were so beautiful later, when she arranged them

on a tray, that I couldn't bear thinking people were going to eat them up the next night.

"How about sampling a couple now?" she suggested before sliding the tray into her immaculate refrigerator.

"Oh no!" I said, and she suddenly burst out laughing when she saw my face.

Uncle Roger came out of his study into the kitchen, sniffing the air. "Fee, fi, fo, fum," he said.

"Out!" my aunt ordered, giggling. "This is for my women's group. He's a compulsive taster," she told me. "We'll have to post an armed guard here tonight to keep him out."

"I always give you some of my french fries," Uncle Roger told her. "I never refused to share my potatoes with you."

"I'm afraid, Izzy," my aunt said, "your uncle has a dreadful secret that you had better be told. He is a nut over french fries." She shuddered. "Especially late at night. So sometimes if you smell greasy, fattening smells in the wee hours of the morning, you'll know who's responsible."

"I like french fries too," I said.

"There, you see," my uncle said to my aunt. "It's a genetic trait—runs in the family. We can't help ourselves. But it could be worse. Some people become werewolves when the moon is full but Izzy and I—we simply take to the kitchen and immerse ourselves in grease." He looked at the clock. "Hmm—9:30, a little early, perhaps, but what do you say, Izzy?"

"I say no," my aunt replied. "She has to get up for school early tomorrow, so maybe we had better work out some kind of compromise." She held out the tray of petits fours. "One," she offered.

"Two," he countered, picking a chocolate square rolled in almonds and an apricot-filled heart with icing.

Aunt Alice took one too and, finally, so did I. We sat in the kitchen eating and talking, nice and easy and relaxed. I could see they both were beginning to feel comfortable with me and it seemed to me that if I could just make them understand that I was a good kid, a happy kid, a kid who wouldn't bother them, they might not send me away.

But first, I had to find Gus.

8

148 Oleander!

Another old lady, but this time one with a bright red mouth and lots of dark eye makeup around her blue eyes and a pile of blonde hair. Maybe it was a wig but it sat up high and yellow on her head.

"Yes?"

"Uh, Mrs. Doyle, I'm looking for the Kaplans. Mr. Holland said I should come and ask you if you know where they are."

She stood looking at me for a second or two, her head on one side. Then she asked it. The question I'd been expecting since yesterday.

"Why aren't you in school, little girl?"

"Oh! Well, it's a holiday and I thought this would be a good time to get in touch with the Kaplans."

"Oh—a Jewish holiday?" said Mrs. Doyle, and I smiled and nodded.

"Are they relatives, dear? Such nice people. Wonderful tenants. Their little boy, Joey, was a real doll. He's not so little anymore. They sent me a picture of him last Christmas. Hard to believe but he's eleven years old now. Little Joey!"

Eleven years old. Just my age. And Mrs. Doyle knows where they are. "No, ma'am, not exactly relatives but I need to get in touch with them."

"Come in, come in," said Mrs. Doyle. "I'll give you their address and I'll show you the pictures of Joey and Danny."

"Danny?"

"The younger boy. Of course, I never saw him. He was born after they left San Francisco but he looks just like Joey, and Myra says they're coming for a visit this summer and she'll bring them both over to see me."

"Where are they, Mrs. Doyle?" I said, feeling scared and almost hearing the roar of oceans between me and Gus.

"New York now. He teaches, you know. Very smart—you wouldn't think it to look at him—a skinny little man with a stutter. But he's been all over—Scotland, France, Chicago, and now New York. She's tired of traveling, she says, and she wants to settle down. Here—I have their pictures right here in this envelope."

Upstairs, a woman began singing and Mrs. Doyle looked up to the ceiling and rolled her eyes. "There she goes again," she said to me. "She promised she wouldn't. I never would have rented her the apartment if she didn't promise. I told her—between one and five I'm gone and you can sing all you like then but not when I'm here." The singing went on and Mrs. Doyle handed me an envelope and said, "Just sit down and look them over, dear. I'll be right back."

She left me alone in the room and I sat down carefully on a very soft chair. I opened the envelope and pulled out some pictures. The first one was of two boys and the others showed the boys sometimes by themselves and sometimes with a woman or a man and sometimes with both. Dr. and Mrs. Kaplan and their two sons, Joey and Danny. I really felt like a close friend of the family. But in none of the pictures did I see Gus.

The singing suddenly stopped upstairs and shortly afterward, Mrs. Doyle returned. "She said she forgot," Mrs. Doyle told me. "So I said to her, 'Miss Sorenson, this morning at 6:30 you also forgot and the day before yesterday, I believe, you forgot at eleven in the evening.' She apologized and said it wouldn't happen again but I don't think she can help herself. You just can't trust those music conservatory students."

She looked at the pictures in my hands and smiled. "The Kaplans were the best tenants I ever had. I hardly ever saw Dr. Kaplan, and the little boy was in nursery school all day and took long naps whenever he was home. Marvelous people!"

"What about their dog, Mrs. Doyle?"

"Their dog?"

"Yes. Their little black dog, Gus. What about Gus?"

"Poor thing!" said Mrs. Doyle. "I don't generally like animals but he was really unusual—such a quiet, gentle dog. I felt so bad for him when they left."

"What happened?" I cried. "Didn't they take him with them?"

"Why, they couldn't take him with them. They were going to Edinburgh and they had to leave him. They felt bad too because he was such a sweet little thing. I would have taken him myself if I didn't have all this good furniture. But a dog is going to chew on things and jump up on furniture and you know what else."

Even though Mrs. Doyle was nothing at all like Mrs. Firestone, I knew how to ask the right question this time.

"Where is Gus now?"

"Was that his name, dear? I didn't remember. Well, they left him with Mr. Bailey over in the dry cleaning store on Aster. I don't think he has him anymore but let me give you the Kaplan's address and when you write to them be sure to send them my love."

Mr. Bailey, said the young woman in the cleaning store, was out making some deliveries and would not return until the afternoon. No, she said, she didn't know anything about a dog named Gus. She only came in twice a week to do alterations but why didn't I come back after one o'clock.

It was 10:45 which meant I had over two hours to get through before returning. What was I going to do for more than two hours? I tried to tell myself that now I really was on the right track but I began feeling worse and worse as I circled around the dry cleaning store and thought about Gus. About how nobody really wanted him. About how every owner had kept him only a little while and then passed him on to somebody else who didn't want him either.

I looked at a clock in a barber shop—eleven o'clock. I knew I'd never last for two hours watching the shop and thinking about Gus. I began walking. What could I do to make myself feel better? I could eat something but it was too early, and in any case, I wasn't hungry. The thought of Gus, little, helpless Gus, being passed from one owner to the next made me angrier and angrier. I wanted to hit somebody. I wanted to scream and yell and say, "What kind of people are you to treat a little dog like this?"

Then I saw the library and hurried inside. There was a woman at the desk who looked up at me and asked, "Why aren't you in school?"

"It's a Jewish holiday," I told her.

"Oh," she said, "I didn't know." Then she smiled at me and went back to her work. I found the children's room and the librarian showed me the section on dogs. For the next couple of hours I read through most of them. I looked at pictures of German shepherds, collies, beagles, and miniature poodles. None of them looked like Gus. Then I read a book on how to take care of dogs.

Mr. Bailey was in the store when I returned. He shook his head when I asked him about Gus. "That wasn't his name," he said, "but it was the dog I got from the Kaplans."

"A little black dog?" I asked.

"That's right—a little black dog but his name was Casper."

"Where is Gus—I mean Casper now? Do you still have him?"

"No," he said, "I don't. It was when the Missis got sick. Casper kept whining and whining. It made me nervous. I guess he knew she was going but I couldn't stand it. I didn't say anything to her—to my wife—but I left Casper with my cousin and later, after she passed away, I didn't want him back. I'm at the store all day so who was going to look after him?"

"Where is Gus now?"

"Why, with my cousin," said Mr. Bailey. "I haven't seen him for a year or so but he was there when I saw him last."

"Is he . . . is he happy?" I asked. But I knew the answer before he began speaking.

"Happy?" said Mr. Bailey. "Well, I don't know that I ever thought about a dog being happy. Casper was a good dog—good for the Missis because he was so quiet and didn't bother anybody. Never jumped up on you or made a lot of noise. Until she got sick you hardly even knew he was there."

"Please, Mr. Bailey," I said, "could you tell me your cousin's name and give me his phone number?"

Mr. Bailey said no. But after I told him about Gus and me, he explained that he and his cousin had argued last time they met. He didn't remember what it was all about but he knew his cousin had been wrong. Still and all, he said, it wasn't right to give people's telephone numbers to strangers, even the numbers of stubborn, intolerant people like his cousin. But he agreed finally to call and ask if I could come and see Gus—only he said Casper.

"Leave me your phone number and I'll call you when I get home. Nobody will be home now at his house."

"Why don't I call you later?" I suggested.

"I won't be home until nine or ten."

"Then I'd better come back tomorrow." I knew that my aunt and uncle would grow suspicious if a strange man called me up or if they heard me talking to somebody on the phone.

I went home and helped Gina vacuum the white rugs in the living room that weren't dirty, and clean off the spotless bathroom fixtures. She said I was a big help and she told me how she met her boyfriend and what her parents thought of him and vice versa.

My aunt said we would have a quick dinner that night since her women's group would be arriving by eight. She made steaks with stuffed mushrooms, baked potatoes, and salad. I guess I must have been wolfing down my food because she watched me, smiling, and said, "I must say, Izzy, just in the few days you've been here, I think you've put on a little weight."

I stopped eating, not knowing whether she approved or not. I had forgotten to eat any lunch that day and I was ravenous. Besides which, my aunt is a marvelous cook.

"Just look at her, Roger. Don't you think she's looking better since she came? Not so pale and peaked?"

My uncle had been thinking of other things but he looked at me and mumbled something in agreement.

Aunt Alice kept smiling. "So, Izzy, how is school? Is everything all right?"

"Just fine," I told her.

"And Miss Ballard? Do you still like her?"

"Oh, yes."

"Have you made any friends?"

"Well, yes. There is this one girl who sits next to me."

"The one who showed you around yesterday?"

"That's right. That one."

"What's her name?"

"Uh—Debbie—Debbie Doyle."

"That's nice, Izzy. And I want you to feel you can invite your friends here anytime you like."

"Okay. I mean—sure, Aunt Alice, I will."

"And she can stay for dinner if it's all right with her mother."

"Great!" I told her. "Great!"

Lucky for me, her mind was on her reading group. We all ate quickly and then I offered to do the dishes.

"That's fine, Izzy, if you don't have too much homework."

"I did it already," I told her.

"Well, then, maybe I'll go and get dressed."

I looked my aunt over. She was wearing a pale beige dress with little ivory-colored flowers and some gold chains around her neck. I wondered what she was going to wear for her reading group.

"And Izzy, I want you to meet all the women in the group. They're eager to meet you. As a matter of fact, if you're interested, you can sit in and be part of the group. We usually discuss a book that deals with some subject of interest to women."

I tried to figure out what she was saying. Did she want me to sit in on her group? I would do anything she wanted even if it meant listening to a bunch of boring women yattering about a boring book.

"Uh, sure, Aunt Alice. That sounds very interesting. But do you want me to get dressed too?"

She inspected my clothing—jeans, pink shirt, pink sweater, and shook her head. "No, Izzy, you look fine. Most of them will come dressed very casually. That's why

I want to get out of my work clothes and into something more informal."

Something informal turned out to be a pair of white pants and a pale yellow sweater both as clean and pressed as if they were brand new.

"You really are a handy little thing," my aunt said, looking over the kitchen when she returned. "I never could do anything in the kitchen until I was married." She opened the refrigerator and pulled out the tray of petits fours. "My mother never let me lift a finger."

"Well," I told her, "Karen and Sandy never minded what I did."

My aunt set the tray of petits fours down and turned toward me that worried look all over her face.

"Izzy," she said, "I didn't mean . . ."

"It's okay," I said quickly, and then I remembered that I wasn't supposed to say okay so I added, "I mean . . . I'm sorry . . . I forgot."

"Oh, Izzy!" She started to laugh and she gave me a quick hug. I helped her set up the table in the dining room and soon her friends began arriving.

There were six of them. I smiled at each one as Aunt Alice introduced us and they asked all the usual questions —how old I was, what grade in school, my teacher's name? . . . I helped Aunt Alice serve the tea and petits fours and then I sat in a chair near the back of the room and pretended to be interested in what they were talking about.

It was a book that made a lot of them angry. I'm not sure why but they felt it insulted women by implying that men were smarter. Something like that.

"It's good that Isabelle is sitting in," one of them said. "Girls have to realize that there's nothing they can't do and it's time they stopped letting men push them around."

Men and women, I thought to myself. Not just men—women too. They're just as bad. Like Mrs. Kaplan and even Mrs. Firestone. They didn't have to give Gus away. I smiled whenever the women looked in my direction but all the time I was thinking of Gus and how mean every body—men and women—had been to him and how far away tomorrow seemed.

My uncle came out of his study and the women stopped complaining about men for a little while to say hello to him. "Izzy—ah—Izzy—could you come here for a second," he said to me.

I followed him back to his study and he closed the door behind him. "Do you want to stay there?" he asked me.

I didn't know how to answer so I said carefully, "I think Aunt Alice wants me to stay."

"Only if you're interested," said my uncle.

"Oh!" I said.

"Aunt Alice wouldn't want you to stay if you're not interested," said my uncle. "And neither would I." Both of us were standing. He was taller than my father and more dignified. He stood there, looking down at me, waiting, but I didn't know for what. Finally, I asked him, "What do you want me to do?"

"That's not the question," said my uncle. "The question is what do you want to do?"

I knew what I wanted to do. I wanted to go to Mr. Bailey's store, to his house, or wherever I could find him. I wanted to get the name and address of his cousin and go see Gus. Once I saw him—well, I didn't know what I would do then but for now I didn't want to be sitting with a bunch of women talking about some boring book, or standing with my uncle looking at me as if I was some kind of criminal on the stand.

"What do you want to do?" he was asking me.

Go get Gus! I wanted to tell him but I couldn't.

"I don't know," I said.

"You could go to your room," he said. "There must be lots of things a girl your age likes to do."

"Oh yes," I agreed. But I stayed where I was, looking at him.

My uncle said, "Is there something on your mind, Izzy? Something you want to say to me? Is there anything wrong?" He shuffled around a little bit and looked over my head. I could see he was embarrassed so I tried to get a big grin all over my face. "No, no," I told him. "Everything is fine, Uncle Roger."

He took a quick look at my grin and he said, very serious, very solemn, "Well, I'm glad to hear that but I want you to know, Izzy, I'm here if you need me. I . . . you . . . uh . . ."

"Uncle Roger," I said, "I'm glad you were there."

"Uh, where, Izzy?"

"At the picnic. That day my mother died. You protected Gus. That was the right thing to do."

"I'm glad you think so, Izzy, but I'm afraid your father . . ."

"My father," I told him. "He didn't want to kill Gus. He was just upset. But I know he didn't mean it."

My uncle nodded his head. Then he said, "Why don't you stay here awhile with me, Izzy? I have a bunch of papers to go through but if you want to get a book and . . ."

"Yes," I said. "I'll get a book. I'll be right back."

I moved carefully around the back of the living room but none of the women noticed me. I picked up a book in the guest room and hurried back to my uncle. He was already deep into the papers on his desk. We didn't talk much the rest of the evening but it felt good just sitting there.

9

Mr. Bailey looked happy to see me.

"Oh, am I glad to see you, uh—what's your name anyway?"

"Isabelle Cummings."

"Well, Isabelle Cummings, you really did me a good turn, yesterday."

"I did?" I said. "Did your cousin say I could see Gus?"

"Yes, you certainly did. You know how I told you my cousin and I were angry with each other. Well, when I called yesterday, even before I mentioned why, as soon as he heard my voice he said, 'Henry, is that you?' 'Sure, it's me,' I told him. 'Well, I'm a big fool, Henry,' he said, just like that. '. . . a big fool and I want to tell you I'm sorry.' 'Well,' I said, 'I'm a big fool too and I'm sorry too.' So now we're friends again, and tonight I'm going there for dinner, and it's all thanks to you."

"I'm glad," I told him, "but did he say I could see Gus?"

"Oh! The dog! Casper!" Mr. Bailey's face fell and I held on to the counter.

"Not such good news about him. I feel bad about that especially since you did me such a good turn. I told John— that's my cousin—this nice, polite little girl is going to be very disappointed when she hears."

"Not . . . not dead?" I cried.

"No, no," said Mr. Bailey. "At least I don't think so. They told him they wouldn't."

"What happened, Mr. Bailey? Please—what happened?"

"Well, it turns out that my cousin's daughter—that's his youngest, Ellen, was the one who took care of Casper. She went off to college this fall and there wasn't anybody to look after him. My cousin and his wife both work and now that their last kid is out of the house they wanted a little freedom. Sometimes they wanted to go away for a weekend and it was always a problem what to do with Casper. But they managed until a couple of weeks ago."

"A couple of weeks?"

"Yes. John said he took Casper out for a walk at night but he didn't bother putting him on a leash. It was dark and just as they were about to go back inside, this big dog came along and Casper got scared and ran out into the street. I'm sorry to tell you this but . . ."

"He was hit by a car," I cried.

"Yes, he was. Not killed, no, but his leg was broken and my cousin and his wife decided it was too much trouble, especially since Ellen wasn't going to be around to look after him."

"I hate your cousin, Mr. Bailey," I shouted. "He's a bad man."

"He's stubborn," Mr. Bailey admitted, "and not always considerate, if you know what I mean, but he's not a bad man."

In my mind, I could see Gus lying there in the street, maybe in a pool of blood, lying there in pain and all alone.

"Where is Gus now?" I cried.

"I think—I hope—at the S.P.C.A. They're really very nice people down there," Mr. Bailey said helplessly. "They told John they'd put a cast on his leg and they would try to find another home for him. They said he seemed to be a healthy dog."

On the bus to the S.P.C.A., I remembered what I had forgotten—Gus's number. But how many little black dogs with casts on were there likely to be. Hurry! Hurry! Hurry! I wanted to cry out, and kept throwing myself forward to make the bus go faster.

When I got there, I hurried into the shelter but they stopped me at the desk. No, they said, I couldn't go inside without a grown-up. But nothing was going to stop me from seeing Gus. Not this time. Not ever again.

I went outside and waited. After a while, a woman with three kids got out of a car and I tagged right along behind them. She stopped at the desk and explained that she was looking for a kitten for her children. "A white kitten," said one of the children. "No, a black one," said another. I stood behind the woman and hoped nobody at the desk would remember me from before.

Nobody did. We all trooped into the shelter together but when the woman and her kids went off into the rooms

with the kittens I separated from them and went looking
for the dogs.

There were rooms and rooms of them. Each one had
seven or eight cages and there were dogs in most of them,
looking for a home. There were big ones and little ones,
quiet ones and noisy ones. Some of them jumped up on
the bars of their cages as I passed and tried to lick my
hands.

It was so sad that I promised myself that one day, when I
was a grown-up and a vet, I would live in a big house with
lots of dogs. I wouldn't care how the house smelled or if
there were dog hairs on all the furniture. It would be a
home, a real home for dogs like the ones I passed, barking
and crying in the S.P.C.A.

I finished all the rooms down one long corridor and as I
stood, hesitating, a young woman came over to me and
said, "Can I help you?"

"Oh—yes—I—uh—my mother is looking at cats but I
wanted to see the dogs. The male dogs. Are there any
other rooms with male dogs?"

She led me down another corridor with more rooms. In
the second one I found him, in the third cage down, sitting at the back, quiet—not barking, not whining, just
sitting there quietly, licking the top of his cast. The card
on his cage said he was seven years old, gentle with children, and that his name was Casper. But I knew who he
really was. My dog. Gus.

"Gus!" I cried. "Gus! It's me."

He didn't move. His ears stood up just a little and he
raised his head but he stayed where he was.

I knelt down by his cage and I called him. "Gus! Gus!

Don't be afraid. I won't hurt you. I won't let anybody hurt you ever again."

Slowly, he pulled himself up and slowly, he limped over to the front of the cage. I put my hand inside the cage but I didn't touch him. He sniffed at my fingers and I said to him, "It wasn't my fault, Gus."

He stood very still, listening. Even when I began stroking his head, he still did not move.

"He's a quiet one," said the attendant as she came into the room. "Not a peep out of him. I guess he's the quietest dog I've ever seen here. People complain a lot about a dog who barks but they sure don't want a quiet one."

"I want him," I said. The fur on Gus's head felt soft and very familiar, like I'd been stroking it for years and years.

"I'm glad," she said, "because he's such a gentle dog and I don't think he's had a very good time of it. I didn't honestly think we'd find a home for him. People looking for a dog don't want a quiet, sad little guy like this one. They want a happy, friendly one the frolics around and looks like fun. This poor dog just sits in his corner all day— he doesn't make a good impression."

"What would have happened to him if I didn't come along?" I asked her.

The woman said, "We like to find homes for all our healthy animals and we do—for over 90% of them. But we also have to make room for animals that keep coming in. We never have enough room."

I knew what she meant. But I had come in time.

She said I couldn't take him with me. She asked me where my mother was so I had to tell her the whole story. She was very kind to me. She said she would take especially good care of Gus until I returned with a grown-up to sign for him. And she promised that nothing would happen to Gus until I returned—with the grown-up. I made her promise a couple of times but she also said I shouldn't wait too long.

I kept thinking and thinking after I left the S.P.C.A. Who? Who? Who? Not my aunt and uncle in their clean white house. Not them. Who in this whole world of millions and millions of people would care enough to rescue one little, quiet, sad dog who nobody ever wanted?

There was only one possibility.

She said no, at first. She said she was too old to go. That she never left her home anymore. It was one thing if people brought animals to her or if cats found their way there but another to expect her to go out herself. When she was younger, yes. Then she could, but not now.

I pleaded with her for a long time. I begged her and she shook her old head but I could see she didn't want to say no and I kept on.

"I'll come every day, Mrs. Firestone. I'll do whatever you want. I'll go shopping for you and I'll clean your house."

"No," she said. "I wish I could but I'm too old."

"You're not too old, Mrs. Firestone. Please, Mrs. Firestone? I'll take care of all the other animals and I'll put fresh water in the pool every day for Franklin and Eleanor."

She kept saying no until I reminded her about how they would kill Gus if she didn't take him.

"Murderers," she cried. "That's what they are—murderers."

"The woman at the S.P.C.A. told me herself. Nobody wants Gus. He's too sad."

"No wonder," said Mrs. Firestone, "after what he's been through. Shame on all those terrible people! Shame on Loretta! Shame on me!"

"They'll put him to sleep," I said. "You can't let that happen, Mrs. Firestone."

"Yes," she said finally. "Yes." And I put my arms around her and smelled her dry old newspaper smell and I loved her at that moment nearly as much as Gus.

It was two o'clock. I hated to leave Gus in the S.P.C.A. one more night but there was no time to go back and get him that day. I told Mrs. Firestone I would return in the morning and I stopped to make a telephone call before getting on the bus home.

Yes, they said at the S.P.C.A., they would expect me tomorrow. Gus would be there, waiting for me, tomorrow.

My uncle didn't make it home that night for dinner.

"He's very busy this week, Izzy," my aunt said, "but he won't forget the date he has with you Saturday."

"Saturday?"

"Yes. Isn't he taking you over to his old neighborhood to see if that old lady who took your dog is still around?"

"Oh—well—he doesn't have to."

"No, he's looking forward to it. And perhaps later, we can have lunch in Chinatown. Have you ever eaten dim sum?"

"No," I said, "but I might be busy this weekend."

"Oh?" she said, and waited.

What was I going to tell her. Nothing about Gus. Not

yet. Not until I had him. Not until he was out of the
S.P.C.A. and safe. Then I would tell her.

"I—uh—I have to do a big report."

"Oh?" she said again. "What about?"

"Uh—the Jewish holidays," I told her.

She nodded her head up and down and looked pleased.
"Well, that's fine and Izzy, if you need to go over to the
public library, Gina can take you tomorrow afternoon. Oh
—no! Gina has to leave early tomorrow. She has a class at
four." She looked at me in a worried way. "She might
even be gone before you come back from school."

"No problem, Aunt Alice."

She really was looking worried. "And then next week,
Izzy, I have to go out of town for a few days. There's an
Indian potter at Taos whose work our gallery is very inter-
ested in. I'll have to be away for a couple of nights and
Uncle Roger will need to go to a meeting on one of those
nights."

"I always stay alone, Aunt Alice. I'm used to it."

"No." Again that worried look on her face. "It's not
right for a girl your age to stay alone at night."

"But my father let me."

Aunt Alice's face looked frozen in worry. "You're too
young. I'll have to find a baby-sitter."

I wanted to tell her if I had a dog you wouldn't have to
worry about me. But what was the use.

I told her I should start work on my report and I went
into the guest room and took the picture of Gus out of the
drawer and looked at it. Gus. Tonight he was all alone in
his narrow cage at the S.P.C.A. He was sitting there in a
corner, sad and lonely, but tomorrow he would have me

and I would make it up to him for all those miserable years.

I looked at the way his tail was wagging in the picture so hard you could hardly see it and it came back to me suddenly how Gus used to go scampering around the house so fast he'd slide on the wood floors. I remembered how I heard him sliding on the floors, first thing in the morning when I woke up, and I remembered hearing something else—the sound of my mother laughing.

It was scary but suddenly I remembered her. I remembered how I used to sit in her lap and how Gus would come flying up to sit in my lap at the same time I was sitting in hers. It made me angry because if my mother hadn't died, none of this would have happened. We would have stayed in San Francisco and every morning when I woke up I'd hear Gus sliding on the wood floors and the sound of her laughing.

"Izzy, do you want a glass of milk?" my aunt asked, poking her head in the guest room.

"No thanks, Aunt Alice."

She looked at me, sitting there with the picture in my hand, and she asked, "How is the report going?"

"Oh, just fine. Just fine. I finished working on it for tonight."

"Well, I'll say good night then. Your uncle will probably be home late. I hope you're not a light sleeper."

"No," I told her. "I'm not."

I heard him. I must have been sleeping very lightly. I remember tossing around a lot and waking up and wishing morning would come and I could go and get Gus. I dreamed funny dreams and a couple of times I woke up waiting for something that didn't happen.

I heard my uncle or I should say I smelled him. I smelled fried potatoes and I jumped out of bed and hurried into the kitchen. It was 2:30 and my uncle, still in a suit and tie, looking very dignified but guilty when he saw me, was frying potatoes. "I'm sorry, Izzy," he said. "I was hoping I wouldn't disturb you."

"I remembered my mother," I told him. "I remembered her tonight. She laughed a lot and she loved Gus."

"Yes, she did," he said, shaking the french fries in the strainer. "And you too. She loved you too."

"He used to slide on the floors," I said. "He was happy then. He barked a lot and he used to wag his tail all the time."

"Have some potatoes," my uncle said.

The potatoes were wonderful—crisp and golden and greasy.

"Did you ever have a dog?" I asked.

"Why sure," he said. "Your father and I, we had three while we were growing up—Buster, Cookie, and Leo. Leo was a beagle and your father liked him the best." He looked at me and said quickly, "It was easy in the old neighborhood. We had a yard and there was a park close by. A dog needs room to run around."

"Yes," I agreed. "That would be a good place for a dog."

He told me about Buster, Cookie, and Leo while we ate our potatoes. Buster ran away and Cookie chewed gum and Leo would howl whenever my father played a harmonica. After we finished, I helped my uncle clean up. We scoured the pan and cleaned every tiny drop of grease off the stove. When we finished, the kitchen looked spotless again and only the smell of fried potatoes remained.

"Good night, Izzy," my uncle said. He put his hand on my shoulder and hesitated.

"Good night, Uncle Roger," I said, and stood a second or two before going back to the guest room.

I fell into a deep, comfortable sleep and woke up happy the next morning. It was time to go get Gus.

10

Something is sure to go wrong, I told myself all the way over to Mrs. Firestone's house. Maybe she's forgotten or maybe she's changed her mind or maybe—she's so old—maybe she died in the night.

When I got off the bus I started running and I was out of breath when I arrived at her house. The cats were arranged all over her yard and Franklin and Eleanor stuck out their necks and hissed at me as I rushed up the stairs.

Mrs. Firestone had not forgotten. She had even dressed up for the occasion and was wearing a funny old hat, a glittery red one with a torn black veil, and was holding a stained white straw purse with big wooden beads.

On the bus, she acted like a little kid. Look at this. Look at that. It had been so long since she'd been out of the neighborhood that she kept pointing out all the changes that had taken place. I listened, agreed, and worried.

Money? I should have enough. I needed $13.25 to get Gus out of the S.P.C.A. and I had brought $43.87 with me, all the money I had. It should be enough to get Gus and buy food for him and maybe pay off some of the debt Mrs. Firestone owed Mr. Holland. So I didn't have to worry about money.

I was worrying about Gus. Would he still be there? They promised me he would, but would he?

He was, sitting there in his corner.

"Okay, fellow," said the attendant, opening his cage, "your friends are here."

Gus blinked at us but remained in his corner.

"Come on, now," the attendant said, "you're going to your new home."

Gus stood up and limped slowly across the cage. He didn't seem happy or excited. Bewildered maybe but not happy.

"Can I pick him up?" I asked.

"Sure," said the attendant. "You don't have to worry about him biting."

I picked him up and held him against me. "Gus," I whispered, "it's going to be okay. From now on, I'm going to take care of you. It's going to be okay."

He was trembling and he didn't stop until we were back on the bus again.

"No wonder," said Mrs. Firestone. "That terrible place scares them. They know."

I felt so happy with Gus in my arms. I put my face down against him and, suddenly, he raised his head and licked my nose.

"Mrs. Firestone," I cried, "he just licked my face. He knows me, Mrs. Firestone."

"Of course he knows you," she said. "Animals know a lot more than people think they know. And they behave better too. I've been disappointed in my life lots of times I can tell you by all kinds of people but animals—I never knew an animal who called me names or threw rocks at me."

She bent over and peered at Gus. "He certainly looks older. Well, that's not his fault. We all get older. Can't help that."

"Thank you, Mrs. Firestone," I said to her. "You've been wonderful. I'll never forget it."

"Oh, that's all right, Izzy. I'm very happy for you and him."

"He won't be any trouble, I promise you. I'll come every day."

"They're none of them any trouble," said Mrs. Firestone. "It's the people who make the trouble."

I carried Gus all the way back to Mrs. Firestone's house and as we walked through the gate, the animals there stood like statues watching us.

"Here's your new brother," said Mrs. Firestone. "Clark, Norma, Errol, Theda, Eleanor, Franklin . . . make him welcome." Poor little Gus began trembling again and Mrs. Firestone said, "He'll get used to them but let's go inside for now. I'll give him some sardines and maybe that will make him feel better."

"But suppose he doesn't like sardines?"

"We'll find something for him to eat, don't worry. I had a cat once who only ate blue cheese."

"I can go shopping, Mrs. Firestone. I have plenty of money to buy him some dog food and maybe I should get him a bed."

"No bed," said Mrs. Firestone. "I'll fix up something for him, don't you worry."

We went into the kitchen and old Spencer stood up unsteadily and started barking.

"Now you stop it, Spencer," said Mrs. Firestone. "I expect you to behave like a gentleman. And you too, Rudolph," she said to the large brown dog who had followed us in. I sat down with Gus in my lap and Rudolph came over to sniff. He didn't seem to find anything wrong because he rested his head, just for a second, in my lap, next to Gus's, let me pat his head, and then moved off, following Mrs. Firestone to the refrigerator.

She put a plate of sardines down on the floor in front of Spencer and a plate of bologna pieces in front of Rudolph. She watched them proudly as they ate. "They're just like people," she said. "Some things they like and some things they don't. You have to respect their tastes."

When I tried to set Gus down on the floor he just collapsed. So I picked him up again and Mrs. Firestone brought a dish of sardines over to him. She held it up to his nose and crooned, "There now, Gus. Try some of these delicious sardines. Build up your strength, dear." A little of the sardine juice spilled on my lap but Gus turned away his face and refused to eat.

"Just be patient, Izzy," said Mrs. Firestone. "You'll see, he'll get used to us."

For a while, it seemed as if she was going to be right. At first, Gus sat in my lap, watching. Then he began stirring. I could feel it and I even was able to set him down on the floor. The other two dogs inched their way over toward him and the sniffing introductions began. Spencer suddenly began wagging his old tail.

"See," said Mrs. Firestone, "he remembers Gus. See how smart he is."

Gus stood still as the other dogs checked him over and then, as they moved off, he seemed almost ready to follow them and to survey his new surroundings.

It was not to be. Through the open door at the back a large, furious cat came charging into the room. She flew over to Gus, arching her back, and screaming at him. Gus turned and leaped into my lap. I could feel his little body trembling and then, from out of his throat came the saddest sound I had ever heard in my whole life—a despairing, defeated howl of terror.

"Oh dear," said Mrs. Firestone, "I forgot all about Loretta."

But Gus had not and there was no way to make him forget. Mrs. Firestone locked Loretta out of the house. She tried to coax Gus out of my lap with tidbits of bologna and pieces of doughnuts. Gus refused to budge. He stayed trembling in my lap, his head buried against me.

"He'll be all right," Mrs. Firestone said. "This time I'll really give Loretta a good talking to. You just leave him here, Izzy, and I'm sure it will work out."

But I knew I could not leave him, not ever again.

Nobody was home when I returned at four o'clock. Gina had already left for her class and the house looked even whiter and cleaner than usual.

I carried Gus into the guest room and held him in my

lap and I told him what had happened to me in the past seven years since they had separated us.

My aunt found us there. I heard her as she came through the front door. "Izzy," she called, "Izzy, are you home?"

"Yes," I said, "I'm home."

I could hear the sound of her steps coming closer and I held on to Gus and waited.

"Izzy," she said, smiling as she came through the door of the guest room, "I wanted to ask you if . . ."

She never asked me. Instead, she froze in place when she saw him. "Oh, my God," she said, "who is that?"

"It's Gus," I told her. "My dog, Gus."

She looked around the clean white guest room, at the white bedspread, at the pigeon-dropping painting, and she said, "He can't stay here."

"I know," I told her. "And neither can I."

Then I began crying. Now, I'm generally pretty careful when I cry. I like to do it when nobody's there to see. And I like to throw a few things around, things I can pick up later and put back in place, like towels or pillows. I don't like to cry in front of other people, but this time I didn't care.

"You're not going to separate us," I told her, hugging Gus against me. "Not anymore. You can send me anywhere you like but he's got to go with me."

"I don't understand," she said, backing away from me. "Where did he come from?"

"I found him," I said. "In the S.P.C.A. They would have killed him if I didn't take him. Because nobody wants him. Nobody ever wanted him."

I was crying so hard I guess it wasn't clear exactly what I was saying. She said, "Izzy, Izzy . . ." and I looked at her in her spotless beige-and-white suit and it made me so angry I yelled, "It's not okay, this time. And I'll say okay as much as I like. It's not okay. You can't make me stop saying okay even if it's not okay."

"Now, Izzy, just calm down!" said my aunt.

But then Gus began whimpering too—not that terrible, scared howl back in Mrs. Firestone's house—but a sort of sympathetic whimper for me. Because he felt sorry for me. He licked my face again and I began crying buckets. I tried to tell Aunt Alice that I would start packing immediately but suddenly she turned around and hurried out of the room. I knew she was going to telephone my uncle so it didn't surprise me when he came flying into my room, all out of breath, maybe a half hour later. I wasn't sitting on the bed anymore. I was packing my clothes and Gus was down on the floor, watching me. When my uncle came charging into the room, Gus hurled himself against me and I picked him up and stood there, still crying.

"What's going on here?" my uncle said sternly. "I was right in the middle of an important meeting and I had to drop everything and rush home."

"It won't happen again," I told him, "because I'm not going to be living here anymore. I'm going away with Gus."

"Where did this dog come from?" my uncle asked angrily.

"Oh, I'll tell you," I said. I was angry too. Even though I was crying, I was angry—at him, at Aunt Alice, at my father, my mother, at Loretta, Mrs. Firestone, the Kaplans, at Sandy, Karen, Mr. Bailey, Jeremy, Mrs. Doyle, and the singer who lived upstairs. I was angry at everybody in the whole world except for Gus.

I was shaking all the time I was talking. And sometimes I was crying so hard my words came out all wet and fuzzy. "Calm down, Izzy," my uncle kept saying and "Pull yourself together." But I didn't stop.

I told him what I thought of him and Aunt Alice and their clean white house and this big world with all its people who had no place for Gus.

When I was finished my uncle said, "Do I understand from what you have said that you have not been at school all this week?"

"Yes," I said. "No, I have not been at school."

"That you have played hookey from school these past four days?"

"Yes, yes, yes!" I shouted.

"That you have deceived your aunt and myself and gone traipsing all over the city and talked to all kinds of strangers knowing that we would never have approved."

"Yes," I said. "You never would have approved."

"And you also knew, Izzy," said my uncle, "that I would have taken you over to see Mrs. Firestone on Saturday. You knew that I planned on helping you in your search. It wasn't as if I said no."

I hugged Gus hard against me. My tears were bouncing off his head. "Saturday would have been too late," I yelled, beginning to hiccup too. "By Saturday he would have been dead."

My uncle moved a little closer. He looked at me standing there, holding Gus, hiccuping, and crying, and you could see he was disgusted. "You know, Izzy," he said, "you deceived us. You acted so meek and mild, like butter wouldn't melt in your mouth. We thought you were a quiet, obedient child—maybe even too obedient."

"Not anymore," I told him. "I don't have to be that way anymore because nobody wants me either. And Gus doesn't have to be that way. Now that he's got me he can be himself. I know what he's really like. I remember. He likes to play and jump around and make a lot of noise. That's what he's really like and now that I found him, he'll be like that again. You'll see. No—you won't see because we won't be here anymore. But don't try to separate us, Uncle Roger. It won't work. He's my dog and I won't let us be separated ever again."

"I think . . . ," my aunt murmured, putting a hand on my uncle's arm.

"You really had us fooled," said my uncle, "but for the time being, until we decide what would be best . . ."

"I've already decided," I told him. "Nobody will ever take Gus away from me again."

"I think . . . ," said my Aunt Alice.

My uncle stopped looking at me and began looking at Gus.

"So don't try!" I yelled. "Just leave Gus alone."

"But," said my uncle, "that isn't Gus."

11

"I remember," said my uncle. "Just take one look at the picture if you don't believe me. Gus had floppy ears like a cocker spaniel."

The little dog nestled in my arms had small, pointy ears like a scotty.

"I don't know where the picture is," I told my uncle.

"It's not Gus," he insisted. "You have the wrong dog."

"No, I don't," I said. "It's the right dog. Mrs. Firestone said so. And he was afraid of Loretta just like he was when he was a puppy. It's Gus."

"It's not Gus," said my uncle impatiently. "All you have to do is find that picture. You'll be able to see very plainly that Gus's ears were different from the ears of the animal you're holding." My uncle's finger was pointed at my little dog. Guilty, said my uncle's finger.

"No," I told him. "It's Gus."

My uncle said, angrily, "Then there's only one way to settle this, once and for all. Take that animal with you and let's go right now."

My aunt came too. She sat quietly in the front seat, next to my uncle, while Gus and I clung to each other in the back. All the way over to Mrs. Firestone's my uncle kept complaining about the important meeting he was missing and about my stubbornness in not facing the facts. I stroked Gus's head and whispered in each of his pointy ears that it was going to be okay.

"No," I told my uncle when we arrived. "I'm not taking Gus into her house. We'll wait here."

"You have to come," my uncle insisted. "I want you to hear what she has to say."

"No," I repeated. "Loretta scares Gus and I'm not going to bring him in there again."

"Izzy!" he said.

"No!" I answered.

"Roger," said my aunt, "I'll come with you and perhaps we can persuade Mrs. Firestone to come back to the car—without Loretta."

It was growing dark but I could see my tall, dignified uncle and my neat, fashionable aunt as they opened the crooked gate to Mrs. Firestone's yard and made their way through the cans and papers, past the two rusty bikes, the lopsided baby carriage, the child's pool filled with water, and Eleanor and Franklin who stuck out their necks and made undignified noises. I watched them as they knocked on Mrs. Firestone's door but I couldn't hear what they were saying when she opened the door and stood there talking to them. Finally, my uncle put out an arm, held

Mrs. Firestone by the elbow, and escorted her over to the car. He opened the back door and said, "If you don't mind, Mrs. Firestone, would you please take a seat next to my niece?"

"Good evening, Izzy," said Mrs. Firestone. "Good evening, Gus."

"He says this isn't Gus," I whispered. "He wants you to say it isn't Gus."

"Nonsense," said Mrs. Firestone. "This certainly is Gus."

My uncle and aunt took their seats in the front of the car, and my uncle cleared his throat.

"I'm very sorry to bother you this way, Mrs. Firestone, but I believe you are the only one who can convince my niece that she has the wrong dog."

"His name is Gus," said Mrs. Firestone.

"There," I said to my uncle. "She said it was Gus. You heard her say it was Gus."

"Yes," said my uncle. "I certainly did. Mrs. Firestone, let me just ask you a few questions."

"Certainly," said Mrs. Firestone.

"Did I or did I not bring you a small black dog about seven years ago?"

"Certainly," said Mrs. Firestone. "I remember it very well."

"What was the dog's name please?"

"Gus," replied Mrs. Firestone.

"Now, would you please," said my uncle, the lawyer, "tell my niece what happened to that dog."

"Well," said the witness, "my cat, Loretta, scared him so I had to give him to the S.P.C.A. I didn't want to but . . ."

"I told you all of this already," I interrupted. "Why are you acting like Gus is on trial? Mrs. Firestone just told you that her cat scared Gus and that she gave him to the S.P.C.A. You heard what she said. And this was that dog, wasn't it, Mrs. Firestone?"

"Certainly," said Mrs. Firestone. "Of course he was a little younger then."

"Yes," said my uncle, "and his ears were different then too, weren't they?"

"Certainly not," said Mrs. Firestone, laughing. "His ears were the same. A dog's ears don't change over the years."

"I shouldn't think so," said my uncle, "but the dog I brought you had ears like a cocker spaniel and this dog has pointy ears."

Mrs. Firestone remained silent.

"Do you remember, Mrs. Firestone, that the dog I brought you had long, floppy ears and his name was Gus?"

Mrs. Firestone wrinkled up her forehead. Then she looked down at the dog in my lap and gently put a finger on one of his ears. "Oh!" she said, shaking her head, "that dog!"

"Now, Mrs. Firestone," said my uncle, "will you kindly tell us what happened to that dog, to the dog named Gus?"

"I don't know," said Mrs. Firestone, looking at me sadly. "I'm sorry, Izzy, I don't know. He ran away the next day. The gate was open and he must have gotten out. He was such a cute little dog and he and Loretta got along just fine. But he must have gotten out and I guess somebody found him—such a cute, lively little dog. Anybody would

want a dog like that. I'm sorry, Izzy, I forgot all about him
—all about that dog."

"Now, then," said the prosecutor, "would you tell us
about this dog?"

"Izzy," Mrs. Firestone said, "somebody else gave him to
me about the same time. Now who was it gave him to me
—not your uncle, no, not him, but it was a man, another
man . . . like your uncle. And right around the same
time—or nearly around the same time, I'm not exactly
sure when. But both of those dogs were black, I'm sure of
that, Izzy, and that's why I mixed them up. I'm sorry,
Izzy."

"Thank you, Mrs. Firestone," said my uncle.

Mrs. Firestone said to me, "Izzy, you know I can't give
Loretta away. She's been in the family too long for that
but I still think I could have a good heart-to-heart talk
with her. She's older now. She'll listen to reason."

"That's quite all right," said my uncle. "It won't be
necessary since I'm sure Izzy will agree this is not Gus."

"No," I told him, hugging my dog closer to me, "this is
Gus. I'll go anywhere you want to send me but you're not
going to take him away from me."

Mrs. Firestone put her bony fingers on my arm. "You
see, Izzy," she said, "it's like this. I'm very old. I don't even
remember how old anymore. But I'm still here and if you
don't have any better place, if nobody will take you—you
and Gus, I mean, you can come and live with me. I don't
generally like children but since you don't seem to have
any other place to go . . ."

"But what about Loretta?" I asked her. "I don't think
she likes me any better than she likes Gus."

"She's not used to children. It won't be easy but I'm sure we can work something out."

"Maybe if Gus and I just stay out of her way most of the time. We're both quiet and we won't bother her."

"Roger!" said my aunt.

I was beaming at Mrs. Firestone and she was nodding her head and beaming at me. I had a place to go. Gus and I. We had a home. "I'll go back and pack my things. I can come back tonight if my uncle will drive me back. Otherwise, I still have some money. I can take a cab."

"But Izzy," my uncle said. "If this isn't Gus, if this isn't the dog you were looking for, why do you want to keep him?"

The little black dog was fast asleep now in my arms. "Because he is Gus even if he isn't that Gus. Maybe that Gus found a family that wanted him but this Gus didn't. Nobody wants this Gus. Only me."

"Stubborn," said my uncle. "Just like your father."

"No," I said, "I'm not like him. I don't want to be like him."

"He was for the underdog," said my uncle. "And so are you."

My uncle helped Mrs. Firestone out of the car and walked her back up the stairs. I could see him talking to her and her nodding and then shaking her head.

My aunt didn't say one word until he returned to the car. Then she turned around and asked me, "Is that dog housebroken?"

"Of course he's housebroken. He's seven years old, isn't he?"

"I don't like the tone of your voice, Izzy," said my uncle.

"I'm sorry," I said, "but it was a pretty dumb question, you have to admit. Anybody knows a seven-year-old dog is going to be housebroken."

She sighed. "I suppose he'll shed all over the place."

"Probably," I said. "He's got kind of long hair but Mrs. Firestone won't mind. Her place is full of cat hairs."

"And who will look after him while you're in school?" my uncle asked.

"Oh, he's used to looking after himself," I told him. "It's Loretta I'm worried about."

"Well, you can stop worrying," said my uncle. "You're not going to live there—I mean you and Gus are not going to live there." His face was serious and solemn. But then he reached back and touched Gus's head.

"And besides," said my aunt with another sigh. "It wouldn't be fair."

"Who to?" I asked. It sounded angry the way I said it and suddenly I realized that they were asking me to stay with them. Not only me but Gus too. In one night, I was getting two offers. I really preferred Mrs. Firestone's but I knew that Gus wouldn't be happy there. It was a big thing for my busy uncle and my busy aunt to let me stay with them. It meant that Gus's black hairs would get all over their white carpets for one thing. For another, they'd have to put up with me. They didn't know anything about kids. Like Mrs. Firestone, they probably didn't even like kids but they were going to let me stay.

And what about me? I'd have to wake up every morning and see that pigeon-dropping painting in my room. Because it would be my room if I stayed. They couldn't ship me off to boarding school with Gus. I felt sorry for them and I thought maybe I could learn to live with the painting. Maybe I could even get to like it. Maybe I could even get to like them.

I should have thanked them. I should have spoken to them in my soft, gentle voice but I didn't.

"No," said my poor aunt, "it wouldn't be fair."

"Who to?" I said, stroking the soft, sleepy head of my dog, Gus.

"To Loretta," she said.